SLAMDUNKED
by LOVE

A ONE-ON-ONE STORY

JAMIE WESLEY

Enjoy!
Jamie Wesley

Entangled Publishing, LLC
2614 South Timberline Road
Suite 109
Fort Collins, CO 80525
Visit our website at www.entangledpublishing.com.

Lovestruck is an imprint of Entangled Publishing, LLC.

Edited by Tracy Montoya
Cover design by Heather Howland
Cover art from iStock

Manufactured in the United States of America

First Edition December 2015

To my mama, who never questioned my sudden obsession with sports when I was 11, even though I wasn't and never would be an athlete. LOL.

Chapter One

*P*ut, put. Eerrrgh. Clunk.

And just like that, Caitlin Monroe's beloved car said, "No more." The side of the road was as far as it was willing to go. It was done. No hope for recovery.

Great.

She dropped her forehead to the steering wheel. Yes, she'd heard the Jetta making weird noises over the past month— okay *months*—but wasn't that what cars did, especially when they were fifteen years old? The vehicle always started and got her where she needed to go. She'd always planned to get it looked at—at some nebulous point in the future when she could bear to part with the money.

Now she was stuck. At least until the tow truck arrived. But who knew how long that would take? She pulled her phone out of her silver clutch and called her roadside assistance company.

"Someone should be there within the hour," the customer service agent said.

Fan-freaking-tastic.

She ended the call, huffing out an impatient breath. Damn it, she had somewhere to be. Someone to confront. Someone to expose.

It was going to be glorious.

Assuming you can go through with it. Caitlin lifted her chin and told that stupid voice in her head to shut up. Of course she could go through with it. She *would* go through with it. She was on the side of right.

But when was she going to get there for her moment of glory? She checked her watch. Only fifty-five more minutes to go until help arrived. "Ugh."

Why weren't things going as planned? Tapping her fingers on the steering wheel, she stared out the window. A few cars zoomed by without stopping. She didn't blame the drivers. They didn't know her from Eve. She didn't want them to stop anyway. She didn't know *them* from Adam. She'd be okay. Downtown Dallas wasn't exactly a beehive of activity on Wednesday nights, but streetlights kept some of the shadows at bay.

Her gaze fell on her phone. No time like the present to find the perfect raspberry cheesecake recipe she was certain existed on Pinterest somewhere.

A few minutes later, her head jerked up at the sound of a car pulling up behind her. But instead of the AAA utilitarian vehicle she was expecting, a low-slung sports car appeared in her rearview mirror. She sucked in a breath. Oh God. She was going to be murdered because she chose to drive a fifteen-year-old clunker.

She quickly double-checked that her doors were locked. And one more time when the door on the driver's side of the—was that a Porsche?—opened and a shiny, expensive-looking black wingtip hit the pavement.

A rich serial killer? Sure, why not? There was no law that said serial killers couldn't be rich. Hell, being rich probably meant they had more resources at their disposal to use to commit their crimes.

Other cars continued to drive by, so hopefully if the other driver did try to kill her, someone would witness the crime. Caitlin shook her head. Wait. Was that really her silver lining in all this? An eyewitness to her demise? *Why* had her car chosen tonight of all nights to crap out on her?

Tap, tap!

Only her seat belt saved her from the indignity of hitting her head on the roof of the car. Porsche Guy tapped the driver's side window again. She stared straight ahead out the windshield. Maybe if she refused to acknowledge his presence, he'd go away.

Or not.

He stepped in front of her car. From this angle, he was standing too close for her to see his face, but she saw that he wore a suit. Long legs. Cufflinks—diamonds?—winked under the streetlight. Then he bent down and waved.

Caitlin's eyes widened. She recognized him. Even through the faint wisps of smoke billowing out from under the hood of the car. Kind of impossible not to if you spent any time on the internet or ever turned on a TV. When he wasn't starring in soda and shoe commercials, his fantastic plays and sometimes caustic soundbites were being highlighted on ESPN.

Brady Hudson. The newest point guard for the NBA's Dallas Stampede.

God, he was hot. Drool-worthy. Fine. And whatever other superlatives came to mind. She took the opportunity to go slow and take it all in. His dark blue jacket hugged broad shoulders. A red tie and crisp, white shirt drew attention to his wide chest. Slim pants accentuated long legs. Her eyes slid up. Black hair cropped close to his scalp. Skin the color of rich mahogany. His eyebrows were drawn together in concern over eyes the color of her favorite dark chocolate.

Sharp cheekbones any woman would kill for only added to his appeal.

Not that she was interested, of course. Just admiring the pretty.

She took a deep breath, her heart rate slowing down. Talking to him should be okay. Yeah, the basketball player had a reputation for being kind of an ass who'd gotten the boot from his last team because he'd never learned how to get along with others, but that was better than having a reputation for being a murderer. She pressed the button to roll down the window. And growled in frustration when nothing happened because the damn car was dead.

Brady rounded the car to her side and peered at her through the glass with those hypnotizing eyes. She eased the door open.

"Looks like you're having some trouble here," he said.

She offered up a small smile. "Yeah, but AAA will be here soon. I'm good."

"Want me to take a look at it?"

"In that fancy suit?" She shook her head. "No, I wouldn't do that to you."

He scanned her figure. "You're dressed pretty fancy yourself. Going somewhere special?"

"Probably the same place you are."

He nodded once. "The team's charity casino night. Right. Makes sense you were on this street." He paused. "So you know who I am?"

She lifted an eyebrow. "Dude, the *only* reason I opened my door was because I recognized you. You could've been an ax murderer."

He chuckled. "Watch a lot of Discovery ID, I take it?"

Her shoulders stiffened. "I do not." He shot her a disbelieving look. "Okay, yes, I do."

He laughed again. "Since you know my name, seems only

fair that I know yours."

She hesitated. It felt a little revealing, a little personal giving him that piece of info. Like they were forming a connection. Which was ridiculous. How many thousands of times had she introduced herself to people? Telling him her name would mean exactly nothing. "Caitlin."

"Ms. Caitlin." Her name had never sounded so sexy rolling off the tongue. He propped his hand on the roof of the car and glanced around before returning his attention to her. "Look, it's dark out here. How about I stay with you until the tow truck gets here?"

Wait. What? Mr. Self-involved was going to stay with a woman he didn't know for who-knows-how-long? "You don't have to do that."

He shrugged. "I know, but you're rubbing off on me. It's dark and quiet. A little scary. I can't leave you out here by yourself." He placed a hand over his heart, his lips tilting upward. "Humor me."

Struck dumb by his winning smile, the answer popped out before she could stop it. "Okay."

He slipped off his jacket and relaxed against the backseat door. Awkward silence filled the air—at least on her part. He looked cool as could be, like it would never occur to him to even *think* about having a worry in the world. Still, she couldn't leave him out there by himself. Well, she could, but that would be rude. He was being nice. With a sigh, she unlocked her seat belt and stepped gingerly out of the car, taking a moment to gather her footing. As cute as her shoes were, she didn't wear spindly, four-inch heels every day. Falling on her butt would be the evening's final indignity.

He straightened from his perch. "I misspoke."

That didn't sound good. She frowned and took a hasty step back. "About what? Being an undercover serial killer?"

He laughed again, drawing her eyes to lips she'd

undoubtedly be dreaming about tonight. Which was *not* okay. Neither was the way he smelled. Like leather and soap. All man. "No, I said you looked fancy. That was an understatement."

He did nothing to hide the appreciation in his eyes. *Don't let the flattery go to your head*. He definitely had game that extended well beyond the basketball court. His love life was featured prominently on celebrity gossip sites. Models, entertainers, and socialites. All beautiful. All temporary. Getting into any kind of entanglement with an athlete, especially one with a reputation for being tempestuous, was nowhere to be found on her bucket list. Been there, done that. Had the scars to prove it. She glanced down at the floor-length, red sheath that hugged her curves. "Thanks."

She moved away to lean on the hood of the car.

A mistake.

He stepped directly in front of her, bringing him and his scent way too close *again* and forcing her to look up at him. Because he was a point guard, he wasn't required to be a giant like most of the other players in the NBA. He was "only" six-three, if memory served her correctly, but he towered over her anyway. Granted that wasn't saying much since she was five-two without heels. If she practiced perfect posture. Even with the heels, she wasn't setting any height records. But looking up at him wasn't exactly a hardship. In any way, shape, or form. He was a fine specimen of a man.

"Caitlin? You okay?"

She started, realizing she'd been staring at his sculpted lips again. And based on the smile that played across said lips, he knew it. Great. Yep, it had been too long since she'd gotten laid. Hell, even kissed. She needed to make an appointment ASAP with Bobby, her battery-operated boyfriend. Because fantasizing about Brady Hudson was a non-starter, even if by some miracle he didn't see her as a charity case.

"Sorry, I spaced out for a second," she said. "You know you don't have to stay."

He crossed his arms, pulling the shirt tight over his biceps. "Yeah, you said that already, but the question is why. Usually women do whatever it takes to get me to stay."

"I'm not a groupie," she fired back.

His eyebrows arched. "Duly noted."

Chill, Caitlin. There was no way he could've known that associating her with groupies, no matter how vaguely, was a particularly sore spot for her. "Sorry," she muttered.

"Don't worry about it." Like he had every right to do so, he settled next to her. Damn, he smelled good. And he probably knew that too.

She breathed a silent sigh of relief when the AAA driver pulled up a minute later and hopped out of the truck. "Somebody call a tow service?" His eyes grew big when he spotted Brady. "Hey, aren't you Brady Hudson? Sorry about the game last night. The ref was so off-point. What was he thinking? You should've gone off on him. I would have. How are you liking Dallas?"

"Thanks for the support, but I can't risk a fine or suspension for referee abuse," Brady said with a slight smile. "I haven't seen much of the city yet."

"Oh, that's too bad. I can show you around if you want. I've lived here my whole life."

"Thanks, but I don't want to put you out like that."

"Oh, it's no trouble at all."

Caitlin not-so-gently cleared her throat.

"Sorry, ma'am," the driver said, finally turning her way. "Let me take a look at the car. I'm Joe, by the way." He raised the hood and inspected its contents. Shook his head and let out a heavy sigh. And then he started telling her everything that was wrong with her car. Which would have been fine except her car-maintenance vocabulary didn't extend beyond "gas," "oil changes," and "tire tread."

"Radiator *something something something*. The fuel pump *blah blah blah*. Yeah, I need to bring it in," Joe said, wrapping up his spiel and slamming the hood shut.

She nodded politely like she understood car-speak. Like he wasn't giving her the worst news possible. "Okay."

The driver hooked her car up to his truck and raised it on the bed. He drove away, leaving her clutching his business card and stranded on the side of the road with only the NBA's biggest Don Juan to act as her rescuer. "Bye, Hans," she said, her spirits sinking as her much-loved car faded away in the distance.

"Who's Hans?" Brady asked, his eyebrows pinched together.

"My car."

"Hans?"

"Yeah. Jetta. Volkswagen. German car. German name."

His brows stayed drawn together. "Sure. Okay."

She gestured to the silver Porsche gleaming under the streetlight. "You're telling me that attention-getter doesn't have a name."

His lips cracked into a small smile. "No, can't say that it does. Ready?"

That got her attention. "Uh, what?"

He hitched one shoulder. "Since we're going to the same place, I'll give you a ride."

"You don't have to do that." She knew she sounded silly, but he unnerved her. She'd felt off-center since they'd made eye contact, and she didn't like feeling that way. Truth be told, she'd felt off-center since she'd found the letter a few days ago that had led to tonight's mission.

Brady spread his hands out wide. "I mean, yeah, I could leave you out here at the mercy of the next mom in a minivan with a machete who drives by, but I'd feel bad."

Caitlin cocked her head to the side, narrowing her eyes. "Are you making fun of me?"

"Now why would I do that?" His face remained impassive, but the slight twist of his lips gave him away.

And had her own mouth twitching in response. "Good answer. I'd hate to have to hurt you."

His dark chocolate gaze swept her figure. "Yeah, with what army? You're five foot nothing without those shoes."

Dutifully ignoring the way her skin tingled under his scrutiny, she thrust out her chin. "I am five-two, thank you very much."

He held up a hand. "My bad. *Clearly* you are five-two. A veritable giant."

"You're laughing at me."

His lips twisted again. "Maybe. Now let's get going, Ms. Caitlin."

He moved to the passenger side of the Porsche and held the door open. She slid in, doing her best not to inhale his scent as she moved past him. Doing her best not to make a fool of herself with her contortions to make sure she didn't touch him. Because caressing—err, *touching* him? Nothing good could come from that.

Brady strode around the car to the driver's side, his athletic grace a sight to behold. He slid in, his broad shoulders dominating the space. Desperate to concentrate on something other than his impressive physique, she asked the question that had been bugging her since he showed up. "Why did you pull over?"

He turned toward her, surprise flashing across his face. "What?"

Caitlin shrugged. "No one would've blamed you if you'd kept going. It could've been a ploy to find my next victim. I could've been holding an ax in my lap."

A rumble of laughter spilled from his lips. Damn, he was

gorgeous. "You're awfully bloodthirsty. You looked like you needed help, and I can take care of myself. Besides, look who I found. A beautiful woman. I'm the lucky one."

Her entire body warmed. He could turn on the charm in an instant. Effortlessly. She'd have to be hella diligent about not falling for it. She side-eyed him. "Please. Save the smooth talk for the groupies you're so fond of. Speaking of, is there going to be someone waiting to pull my hair out when we get to the hotel?"

She was making small talk, that's all. Joking. She didn't really care if he had a girlfriend.

A shadow crossed his face, but his lips curved up. "No, I've only been in town a couple of weeks, trying to get acclimated to a new team, a new city. I haven't had any time for dating. What about you? Am I going to have a talking-to from some guy who doesn't know he's supposed to pick up his date?"

She laughed. "No, I'm a free agent. No one's waiting for me." No, it was the other way around. She'd planned to lie in wait for someone else. But the night was still young. No need to abandon her mission just yet.

"Want to play blackjack?" Brady asked, strangely unwilling to part company with the woman he'd spent the better part of the last hour with. As small as Caitlin was, he got the sense she could and would handle herself in any situation she found herself in.

And that intrigued him. *She* intrigued him.

Surprise and something else—uncertainty maybe?— flashed in the pretty brown eyes that dominated her face. She scanned the room like she was looking for someone.

"Thanks, but I'm okay. I'm sure you have better things to do than babysit me," she said, brushing aside a lock of the shiny black hair that swung near her ears in a style that managed to be both cute and edgy.

He dismissed the wave of disappointment that rippled through him. No one liked to get turned down even if it was a casual invitation, that's all. "Okay. I guess I'll see you around."

He didn't move, however. Not even when she said, "All right" and turned away. He shook his head. Why was he standing there like a geeky teen boy who couldn't work up the nerve to talk to his crush? He spun on his heel and promptly bumped into someone.

"Sorry," Brady said automatically, then nodded stiffly when he saw that he'd run into Lance Maguire, the Stampede's starting shooting guard. His backcourt mate. Usually the main recipient of his passes. Always his main detractor in the locker room. Maguire didn't like that his best friend got traded to make space for Brady.

Although this was a social occasion, eyes and ears were everywhere. If it was reported that the two teammates had obviously gone out of their way to avoid each other, it would hit Twitter in two seconds flat, then ESPN in five seconds, and be the topic of conversation on every sports talk show in the city and every other national show tomorrow. No thanks. Maguire was a veteran. Even though he'd made it clear he resented Brady's presence on the team, he knew how to play the media game. Brady held out his hand. "Hey, what's up?"

"Nothing." Maguire didn't bother to make eye contact. Hostility, barely banked, permeated the air. Maybe his teammate *didn't* know how to play the game.

Dropping his hand to his side, Brady bit back a sigh. "Have you tried any of the games yet?"

"Lost a few rounds of poker. The charity will be happy. You look happy." Maguire finally met his gaze. Resentment twisted his features. "Shame considering you cost us the win last night."

Brady suppressed a curse. Did Maguire really want to do this now? After *not* addressing the issue after the game? "You know that's not true."

"Hey, Lance," Dante Whitmore, the starting small forward, said, joining them. He and Lance man-hugged. Brady barely rated a nod. "What are we talking about?"

"Our loss yesterday," Maguire said.

"Oh." Whitmore didn't bother hiding his scowl. "Yeah, that sucked. We should've won."

"We would have if Hudson here hadn't decided to commit a charge instead of passing to me. Maybe he was too busy deciding which Stampede dancer he was going to hit on after the game to notice the guy in front of him."

Fury grabbed Brady by the throat, but he didn't let it choke him. Instead he bared his teeth in a piss-poor facsimile of a smile and peered directly into Maguire's eyes. "This is not the time or the place. Got it?" His voice carried no farther than the three people involved in the conversation, but he made damn sure the steel in his tone came through loud and clear.

Maguire smirked. "Whatever you say. Let's go," he said to Whitmore. The two walked away without looking back.

Still struggling to reel in his anger, looking neither right nor left, Brady headed for the exit. He pushed the door open with more force than necessary and stepped outside. What the fuck was that? Was his time in Dallas destined to be a disaster? As targeted an attack as it was, he could get past the dumbass comment about dancers, but calling his game, the single most important thing in his life, into question? Unacceptable.

The urge to punch something, *someone*, had his hand curling into a fist.

The door opened behind him. Had Maguire followed him out here for round two? Brady spun, more than ready for another confrontation. Caitlin stood there. "Hey," she said softly. "I was coming back to find you and I overheard. That was…brutal."

He uncurled his fist. *Calm down, Brady*. He shrugged. "It is what it is."

"Still." She paused, her eyes full of concern. "I know we just met, but do you want to talk about it?"

"No." Curt would be the best way to explain the tenor of that response even to his own ears. And rude, especially since she'd gone out of her way to check on him, a person she'd known for an hour. He sighed. "I've been driving myself crazy picking apart every play trying to figure out what went wrong. I made the right play."

"You played hero ball."

His lips turned down. "Say what now?"

"You played hero ball," she repeated, obviously uninterested in sparing his feelings.

"How exactly did I play *hero* ball?" he practically growled.

She swallowed like she'd recognized she'd poked a bear looking for its next meal, but she didn't back down. "Well, on the last play of the game, you barreled to the basket all out of control instead of passing to your open teammate in the corner."

"A layup is always a safer bet than a three-pointer." He leveled the glare that always made grown men a foot taller than him toe the line on her.

She didn't falter, her huge eyes remaining clear and focused. "True, except for when you get called for a charge."

"It wasn't a charge. It was a block."

"That's not how the referees saw it."

"It wasn't a charge," he said succinctly. "The game shouldn't have come down to that play anyway. We had an eight-point lead going into the fourth quarter. We blew it." Against his will, his shoulders drooped under the truthfulness of the statement. Damn, he hated losing. Almost more than he loved winning. Losses ate at his soul. Kept him up late at night.

"Well, you have another game tomorrow, so snap out of it."

Despite his shitty mood, Brady found his head lifting, found himself smiling, the intensity of the past few minutes draining out of him in a rush. Usually, people lined up to follow his orders. Caitlin didn't look the slightest bit intimidated. No, she looked like temptation wrapped in a red dress he'd be seeing in his dreams for the foreseeable future. "Yes, Ms. Caitlin. So you're a big fan of the team, huh?"

"Duh. You think I pulled what happened last night out of my butt?"

And what a fine butt it was.

Wait. No. He wasn't supposed to be thinking of her that way. Yes, she was attractive, more than, okay a *lot more* than, but he'd committed to putting his well-chronicled love life on the backburner while he concentrated on basketball and winning the championship that had eluded him his entire career, especially after his last relationship blew up in his face. Women had always been his downfall. No, that wasn't true. Ultimately, *he* was his downfall. He loved women. Their minds. The way they talked. The way they walked. The way they smelled. Too much apparently because more than once he'd let common sense fly out the window when it came to women and lived to regret it. Over and over, they'd proven it wasn't him they loved. It was the money, his status.

So he was putting himself and his goals first. No women. Just basketball.

Then what was the earlier flirting about? his inner bullshit meter countered. *Telling her she looked better than fancy? That* you *were the lucky one?* Just small compliments to make her feel more comfortable with him. *Yeah, right*, the bullshit meter whispered. Caitlin did look beautiful with her shining brown eyes, pretty sienna-colored skin, and red lips. The dress that contoured to shapely legs that would look great wrapped around his waist while he made love to her.

And there he went again. His heart rate increasing, his pants becoming a little tighter. He needed a distraction. "No, it's clear you didn't pull that out of your butt. Ready to go back in?"

He placed his hand at the small of her back. A mistake. An electric charge traveled up his arm. Their eyes met and held. Something hot sparked in her eyes. The moment stretched for a second, two, three. His gaze dropped to her enticing lips. It wouldn't take much effort on his part to bridge the gap between them and stop wondering how they tasted. Wonderful, no doubt.

Only a shout of laughter from behind him stopped him from finding out.

She backed away, nervously tucking her hair behind her ear. "You know I think I need to refresh my lipstick. You don't have to wait for me."

She was offering him a reprieve. Which he would take because he wasn't her date, and that's all there was to it. "All right. Guess I'll see you later."

"Okay," she said slowly, continuing to step away.

Panic seized him. "Caitlin, wait," he called out. "Why were you looking for me?"

"Because I forgot to thank you for stopping to help," she said. "So thanks. I owe you."

"I know," he said.

That stopped her in her tracks. An eyebrow lifted, while her hands landed on her waist. "You do?"

"I do," he said, unable to resist the urge to tease, to challenge her.

Her eyes flicked up and down his body. "We'll see."

Then she spun on her heel and disappeared down the hall, leaving him fighting the urge to grin. Fighting the urge to go after her. But he couldn't, *wouldn't* give in to his baser instincts. No matter how much the curve of her ass in that dress enthralled him. So he returned to the ballroom and headed straight for the bar.

Ten minutes later, after signing a few autographs for fans, he found himself nursing a beer and scanning the crowd. No, he wasn't waiting for Caitlin to reappear. He couldn't be. He was here to make good with the team, not pick up a woman. Prove to the assholes in the media he wasn't a troublemaker. He wasn't. Much. He just liked doing things his way. His way got things done.

Someone tapped him on the shoulder. He turned, expecting another fan. Instead, Elise Templeton, the team's assistant general manager, greeted him with a bright smile. "Brady, hi."

"Hello," he said with a pleasant smile. Inside, he cursed.

He didn't know Elise well. He'd met her right before his introductory press conference with the team. After the press conference, they'd had lunch with the team owner, the general manager, and his agent. She knew her stuff, sharing her insights to his game and how he would fit in with the team.

She'd also felt him up under the table.

"Having fun?"

"Yes," he said politely, because despite what the media claimed, he did know how to be polite.

"That's good, but it is your first time at Stampede Casino Night. You probably need someone to show you the ropes. I'd be happy to offer my services." Elise's lips curved into a smile clearly meant to entice.

The "damns" flying through his head escalated to good, old-fashioned "fucks." *Why* hadn't he abandoned his post a few minutes earlier?

When her hand had landed somewhere it damn well shouldn't have at lunch, he hadn't reacted visibly, at least not above the table, even though he'd come close to spitting out the water in his mouth. He *had* reached under the table and matter-of-factly removed her hand from his inner thigh. They'd run into each other a few times since then, mostly pre or postgame, but he kept the contact brief. Not that a woman needed much time to let a man know she was interested. As she had with flirty glances and lingering touches. But she couldn't do more than that with others around.

She flicked a lock of curly black hair over her shoulder and placed her hands on her trim waist. Invitation shone from her brown eyes. In another time, in another *stupider* time, hell yes, he'd have taken her up on her offer and damn the consequences. But now? He had no desire to mix business with pleasure with a team official, who, yeah, also happened to be the team owner's daughter.

After the confrontation with Maguire, it was abundantly clear that last night's game hadn't helped his stock with teammates, who didn't fully trust him or his objectives yet. If he walked around with Elise on his arm, he knew what they'd be wondering. Was he there looking to find the next woman to add to his list of conquests? Or worse, get in good with the team owner, who'd take his side in any dispute or offer up a large contract in the offseason? Did he not give a damn about the team's success?

"That sounds great, but I can't take you up on that offer," he said to Elise.

"Why not?" she cooed.

"Because…" He had to let her down gently. She was the owner's daughter after all. A splash of color behind Elise caught his eye. He stepped around her and curled a hand around Caitlin's small waist, drawing her to his side. "I already have a date. Elise, please meet my girlfriend, Caitlin."

Chapter Two

Wait. What?

Caitlin froze. Had Brady said what she thought he said? She opened her mouth to say, *"Have you lost your mind? Get off me!"* when he stepped in front of her, his back to the woman who looked like she was contemplating the best way to skin Caitlin alive. His eyes pleaded with her. She pressed her lips together, steeling herself against the ploy. Damn it— why did she keep finding herself involuntarily drawn into his orbit? She knew better. This was *not* why she'd come here tonight. To get involved with some athlete's drama. She had her own drama to deal with, thank you very much.

She opened her mouth again to tell him she wanted no part of whatever he was up to. Only to have his mouth land on hers. He lingered only for a second, but that small taste was enough to scramble her senses. To send a wave of arousal crashing through her.

"Please go along with this. Please," he whispered in her ear. "Sweetheart, I've been looking for you," he said in a louder voice.

Which brought her right back to the real world.

"Well, *sweetheart*, here I am," she answered, her tone as dry as unsweetened chocolate cake.

He sent her a look of censure before turning back to the other woman. "Caitlin, this is Elise."

"It's nice to meet you," Elise said. Considering the way she said it, like the words tasted like vinegar, Caitlin very much doubted the truthfulness of the statement.

"Likewise," Caitlin said as pleasantly as she could.

"How did you and Brady meet?" Elise asked. "He's only been with the team a few weeks, and I'd remember if you were at his press conference."

"Elise is the team's assistant GM," Brady said.

No time like the present to tell the truth. "My car broke down, and Brady pulled over to help," Caitlin said cheerfully.

Elise's lips curved into a stiff smile. "It was your lucky day."

"Indeed it was." Caitlin wrapped her arm around Brady's waist and pinched him as hard as she could through his jacket. Too bad he didn't react.

"Hmm. Well, I don't want to keep you two. I'll be seeing you, Brady. You, too, Caitlin." Elise patted Brady on the forearm, lingering far too long considering his "girlfriend" was standing less than twelve inches away. She swanned through the crowd on the sharpest stilettos Caitlin had ever seen, her head held high.

Caitlin lifted an eyebrow at Brady.

He had the decency to look embarrassed at least. "Don't say anything. Not yet."

Grabbing her hand, he scanned the room and headed toward an exit. Since he outweighed her by Lord-only-knew-how-much, she was wearing shoes that weren't known for their traction, and she was, you know, nosy, she chose not to pull away.

They escaped through a side door into a brightly lit corridor devoid of people. Down the hall, dishes rattled. They'd come through a service entrance. He let go of her hand. Ignoring the way it still tingled, she crossed her arms across her chest and tapped her foot. "Would you care to explain what that was about, *sweetheart*?"

"Remember how you said you owed me?" His lips had the nerve to stretch into a wide, self-satisfied grin. "I'm calling it in."

Her mouth dropped open. "You do realize you can't just *call it in*, right?"

"Oh, I believe I can, and I am." His tone dared her to turn him down. Dared her to argue that going out with him wasn't her most-desired wish.

Now this was the arrogant Brady Hudson who dominated the headlines. She could either order his cocky ass out of her way and leave him hanging or try to figure out what was going on. Her inherent curiosity led her to stop imagining kicking him in the shin and to choose door number two. She directed a no-nonsense look at him. "I need you to back up. What's going on?"

He cleared his throat. "Elise has made her interest in me known. Getting involved with the owner's daughter is not a good idea. I needed a reason to turn her down, and you were there."

Caitlin covered her mouth with her hand to hide a snicker. "Poor Brady. So irresistible. But why would she come on to you?"

He shot her a narrowed-eyed glance. "You are so good for my ego."

She shrugged, still struggling to hold back her laughter. "I have a feeling women have been good for your ego since before you were born. You have to admit it's strange. It can't be good for her professional reputation to date a player."

"I don't think she gives a damn." He scrubbed his face with a hand. "I can't have this happen again."

Again? Caitlin sobered in an instant. "What's going on?"

Brady let out a heavy sigh, his shoulders drooping. "Look, my last girlfriend danced for my old team, and I didn't realize what a big deal it was until the shit hit the fan. People thought I was getting special treatment and resented me for it. Breaking team rules was the excuse the team used to trade me. Dating or even looking like I'm thinking about dating someone who works for the team is the last thing I need. I *need* things to go right here." He lifted his head and wiggled his shoulders like he was shaking off the moment of vulnerability. "So will you do it?"

She cocked her head to the side. "Do what exactly?"

"Pretend to be my girlfriend for a week or two."

Shock reverberated through her, causing her to stumble back a step. "Are you serious?"

"Yes." A self-satisfied grin broke across his too-handsome face like he'd just solved all the world's problems.

"No." Not in a million years. She wanted to get involved with an athlete like she wanted Hans to never get well again.

"Come to a game or two," he continued like she hadn't spoken. "You like basketball. It won't be a hardship."

She threw her hands up. "Which part of 'no' do you not understand?"

"All of it. You don't get anywhere in life by believing you can't succeed."

"Well, it's time to start learning. Besides, you barely know me."

"I know you're not a stage-five clinger. If you were, you'd be jumping at this opportunity."

She would not laugh. "How do I know *you're* not a clinger? If we look at the current situation…"

He went all huffy, arrogant male. "I'm Brady Hudson. I

don't cling."

"Except when you're trying to escape a woman's evil clutches."

"It'll be fun," he said, ignoring the fact that she'd delivered a grade-A comeback.

Again, she jerked back in surprise. "How do you figure that?"

"You get to hang out with me. It'll be our little secret. We'll have fun. Be a little bad. Come on. You know you wanna." A cocky grin accompanied the declaration.

"I do?" She would not return the smile. She would not get sucked in by a pretty face. By a man who had charm for days.

"Please." The cockiness disappeared, replaced again by the vulnerability she was sure he hated to reveal. "I can't flat-out reject her. This will save me a lot of problems. I'm the new guy, and I want my time here to go well. I don't want people drawing comparisons to what happened in New York. This is the easiest way, and I wouldn't ask if it wasn't important."

Caitlin sighed, her defenses collapsing like an undercooked soufflé. Man, she was the biggest sap. "I tell you what. I'll do this for you tonight *only*."

Just like that, the arrogance was back. "I'll take it, but don't be surprised if I change your mind."

"Not going to happen. I'm stubborn. Let's go." Despite the distraction named Brady, she hadn't forgotten the real reason she was here.

After reentering the ballroom, she kept her eyes peeled out for her prey. The room was crowded with fans, players, team staff, and event staff. The night was certainly a success from a fundraiser point of view. As they made their way around the room, people—fans mostly—kept coming up to Brady, one after another, to let him know they were thrilled to have him on the team. While he signed autographs and took photos, she did her part, smiling and playing the doting girlfriend, all the while scoping the room for one particular face.

Behind her, Brady said, "Hey, how are you? It's good to see you." She turned in time to see him shake the hand of the Stampede head coach. Brady drew her close to his side. "Coach, I'd like to introduce you to my girlfriend, Caitlin. Caitlin, the one and only Mack Jameson, the best point guard to ever play the game and the man who's going to lead the Stampede to a championship."

Mack slapped him on the back. "You work fast, Hudson. You've only been in town a few weeks. It's nice to meet you, young lady."

"It's nice to meet you, too." Somehow, she managed to speak normally. She didn't know how.

After all, she'd just spoken to her father for the first time in her life.

Now was the chance she'd been waiting for since she found the get-lost letter Mack had written her mother so many years ago. The chance to tell him what a coward he was for abandoning her mom and never acknowledging his kids. The chance to embarrass him in front of his colleagues like he so deserved. She opened her mouth to do just that, but the words refused to come out.

Brady studied Caitlin. Ever since they'd talked to Mack, she'd gone unnaturally quiet. Not that he could claim to know her well, but her smile, as sarcastic as it could be, had disappeared. So had the spark in her pretty eyes.

"Want to play blackjack?" he asked.

She tucked a strand of hair behind her ear. "Sure."

"I'll try to go easy on you."

Her eyes narrowed in annoyance like he'd known they

would. "No need. I think I know how to count to twenty-one and how to play the odds. Let's go." She strode away without waiting for him. He followed, holding back a smile. They arrived at the nearest blackjack table as another couple was leaving.

"Perfect," she said.

"Yep, perfect for your decimation."

She sniffed. "Not going to happen."

They played hard and fast, only stopping a few times when fans and a few teammates came up to the table. Losing wasn't in his DNA, but it didn't matter. What Caitlin lacked in skill, she more than made up in moxie, outfoxing him more than once on sheer daring alone. Finally, he held up his hands in defeat. "Caitlin, you're killing me."

"I know," she said with a wicked smile. He sucked in a breath, her shining eyes drawing him in. It took a hard slap landing on his back to jolt him out of his trance.

"How's my newest player?" boomed the Stampede's team owner, Dale Templeton. By the time the man stepped in front of Brady, Brady had pushed his lips into a smile. Dale wasn't a bad guy. He'd had the good sense to approve a trade for Brady after all, but he apparently believed they were best friends and never failed to talk Brady up in the media, even when there was no reason for it. Which only made his teammates more suspicious that he was a me-guy.

Brady offered his hand. "Good, Mr. Templeton. This is a great party."

Dale's hearty handshake matched his stout figure. His walnut complexion and curly black hair he wore in a close cap around his head matched those of his daughter. "It is, isn't it? The Stampede only put on the best events." He shook his finger at Brady. "But hey, I've told you a million times to call me Dale."

Brady nodded, contrite. "You're right. My apologies."

"No worries. Why don't you introduce me to your date?"

"Of course." Brady drew Caitlin closer at the waist, ignoring the way his hand felt right at home. "Dale, I'd like you to meet Caitlin."

"Nice to meet you, Caitlin. You must be something if Brady brought you."

"I don't know about all that, but I do my best," Caitlin said.

"Daddy, there you are," a new voice joined in. Elise. "Oh, hi, Brady, I didn't see you there. Caitlin."

Caitlin, to her credit, didn't wilt under the paltry greeting, merely offering up a polite smile. "Elise, hi. I was just about to tell your father I've always wanted to meet the man who saved the Stampede from being the league's laughingstock."

Seemed his date came to impress. Year after year, the team had found itself in last place in its division. Until Dale bought the team a few years ago with the millions he'd earned with his chain of soul food restaurants. He'd invested in the team by hiring Mack and spending the money to bring in a higher quality of player, risks that had paid off. Except in one area. The team hadn't won a championship yet. But they would if Brady had anything to say about it.

"Thank you," Dale said before turning to Brady with a nod of approval. "You hang on to this one, Hudson. She knows her stuff and how to give a compliment without sounding like a complete suck-up."

Brady and Caitlin joined the owner in companionable laughter. Elise could only offer up a pained smile.

"I have to mingle." Dale slapped him on the back again. "Come with me. Let me introduce you to some of our season ticketholders."

Brady found himself sandwiched between Dale and Elise, who wasted no time pressing herself against his side. He glanced behind him and mouthed, "Help me." Caitlin hid her laugh with her hand and offered up a shrug. He faced forward again and immediately wished he hadn't. A few feet away, Maguire met his gaze, doing little to hide his disgust. Brady lifted his chin, refusing to break eye contact until Dale tugged on his sleeve.

He pushed aside all thoughts of Maguire and turned his attention to greeting fans. A few minutes later, after the group dispersed, he made his way back to Caitlin. "Sorry about that."

She waved a hand. "No worries. I understand your adoring public awaits."

He studied his pretend date, struggling *again* not to laugh. "You're not going to cut me any slack, are you?"

She shook her head in mock remorse. "No."

Brady couldn't hold back his laughter any longer. He placed his hand over his heart. "You're so kind."

She nodded solemnly, her eyes twinkling. "I know."

"Since you're so wise, what do you think about getting a drink?"

"I think that's a great idea."

They hadn't gotten far when someone else slapped him on the back.

Ryan Tillerson, one of the few teammates who'd been welcoming to him, stepped into Brady's line of sight. "Brady, my man, you got here. With a date," he added, eyeing Caitlin.

Brady resisted the urge to roll his eyes at the nosiness Tilly was doing nothing to hide. "Ryan Tillerson, meet Caitlin Monroe. Caitlin, Tilly, my teammate."

"Hi, it's nice to meet you," she said.

"It's my pleasure, believe me," the troublemaking Tilly said in a smooth tone he would undoubtedly categorize as charming. "I wish I could say I've heard a lot about you, but that would be a lie."

Caitlin quickly glanced at Brady. "We haven't been, umm, dating that long."

"Good. Then you won't mind dumping Grumpy Cat and coming to have some fun with me. Look at how he's scowling."

Brady knew Tilly was trying to get a rise out of him. He didn't care. He didn't know why he didn't care. He just didn't. Brady stepped between his teammate and his pretend girlfriend. "Not going to happen, Tillerson. Get your own woman. Oh, wait. Don't you already have one?"

Tilly's green eyes laughed at him. "For the night, yes. But you can't blame a man for noticing a pretty lady. Speaking of my date, she's beckoning frantically. Must be something good." Tilly wiggled his eyebrows and disappeared into the crowd.

"He's funny," Caitlin said.

Brady grunted.

Her eyebrows lifted. "What was up with that whole 'get your own woman' deal? We're not actually dating, remember?"

Yes, he remembered. "I know this isn't real, but I also don't appreciate someone else trying to poach the woman I came with, especially when he has a date." Brady divested an approaching waiter of two flutes of champagne and handed one to Caitlin before taking a swig of his own drink, the cool liquid doing nothing to calm his ire.

She took a sip of her champagne. "I'm pretty sure he was joking, but okay," she said over the top of the glass. "Not that it matters. I wouldn't date him anyway." She made a dismissive wave with her free hand.

Curious, he lowered his glass and studied her. "Why not? He's rich, not bad to look at, a good guy." Why was he extolling the virtues of another man? Because although she was talking about Tilly, it felt like she was talking about him. And he wanted to know why. He might not be interested in dating right now, but rare was the woman who had no desire to date him. Especially one he found…interesting.

She shrugged. "Not my thing, that's all."

His head tilted to the side. "Not your thing? What does that mean?"

"You don't want to get into that. Let's play blackjack."

He held up a hand. "No, I want to know."

She took a deep breath. "Well, since you asked, athletes don't have the best reputation when it comes to relationships."

"So you're just going to lump us all in together?"

Caitlin's shoulders hunched in. "I have my reasons."

Like what? Before he could ask, she stepped up to the blackjack table and asked the dealer for some chips. Brady followed and tried to push their conversation out of his mind. This wasn't real. It was just for the night, so her anti-athlete stance didn't matter. He wasn't looking to get involved with anybody anyway.

An hour later, after he'd "donated" all the cash in his wallet to the cause, his date again showing him no mercy, he shifted toward her. "Are you ready to go? The party is slowing down."

She glanced around the ballroom, which was now only half full, her hands twisting at her waist. "Umm…"

He frowned. "Did you forget something?"

She faced him, biting her lip. "No."

Okay, but *something* was bothering her. "Are you freaking out because I offered to take you home?"

A faint smile curved her lips. "No, I'm about ninety-seven percent sure you're not a serial killer."

"Then what's the problem?"

She shook her head. "There's no problem. Let's get out of here."

He wasn't sure he believed her, but he let it go. They weren't dating, and she didn't owe him anything. They made their way out of the hotel to the valet stand. He handed his ticket to the attendant, who ran off.

"Quite a night, huh?" she asked, collapsing on the bench

next to the stand. She crossed her legs, the slit in her dress giving him a too-tempting glimpse of her thigh.

He loosened his tie, his need for air sudden and desperate. Throughout the night, he'd managed to not think about how much she affected him by concentrating on blackjack and meeting fans. But now they were alone. "You can say that again. Scoot over."

She looked up at him with a sly smile. "Why? I like having the bench all to myself."

"I've gotten a crook in my neck looking down at you all night. This is too much of a difference for me to take." He sat next to her, careful not to look at the bared flesh. Careful not to touch.

Indignation settled on her face. "I'm not that short."

He loved riling her. She made it so easy. Somehow he managed to hold back a grin. "Yeah, compared to a five-year-old."

She snorted. "You must give lessons on how to flatter a woman."

"I do. I give other lessons, too."

"Oh, yeah, like what?" Her lush mouth called to him yet again.

Before he could think about stopping himself, he leaned in and said, "How to treat a woman right. How to make a woman feel better than she ever has before."

She met his gaze squarely, but her voice came out shaky. "Don't try that on me. I'm immune."

"You are?"

"Yep. Sure am." A jerky nod accompanied the statement.

He reached up and brushed aside a strand of hair blowing against her cheek, his fingers lingering against the soft, fragrant skin. His eyes searched hers.

Her eyes darkened, but to her credit, she didn't back away. "What are you doing?"

"Trying to figure you out."

"I'm just me," she whispered.

"That's what I find so intriguing."

Her lips parted, like she was having trouble drawing in breath. The Texas November night air was still sultry, yes, but that wasn't why she was having trouble. He wanted, needed to kiss her. Taste those lips that had been taunting him all night. He lowered his head. And touched nothing but air.

"What's taking the valet so long?" Caitlin asked, looking in the direction of the garage.

Brady blinked, struggling to come out of the trance she'd put him in. "Wh—?"

Caitlin's mouth landed on top of his, cutting off his question. Desire, which he'd managed to keep in check up until now, stormed through his defenses like he did on a breakaway to the basket. She tasted sweet, like champagne and the strawberries she'd nibbled on throughout the night.

All the reasons why he shouldn't, *couldn't* start something with her no longer mattered. He couldn't remember them anyway. Now that he'd had one taste of her, he wanted more. He wrapped his arms around her waist and hauled her closer until she was draped across his chest, her scent, that of peaches, clouding his senses. His tongue teased her bottom lip until she opened up with a moan that fed his desire. He slipped inside, dying to get more of the taste that was driving him out of his mind. Delicious. Sweet. So damned good.

She was right there with him, her talented lips and tongue enticing him to deepen the kiss, pressing her lithe body against him, sending blood rushing to his lap. What was she doing to him? He teetered on the edge of a cliff. Only the sound of an approaching car stopped him from falling over.

Slowly, reluctantly, they drew away from each other. Arousal swirled in the depths of her brown eyes. Arousal that matched his own.

His pulse beating hard in his ears, he gulped for air. Desperate to regain some control, he cleared his throat and asked, "What was that about?"

"Elise was watching." A wicked smile curled her alluring lips. "That was my last act of goodwill as your girlfriend."

Chapter Three

*S*he'd rendered Brady speechless. Better to concentrate on that rather than on how her lips still tingled. Or how her heart still galloped out of control. Or how his gaze, so completely focused on her, so carnal, made her shiver uncontrollably.

She needed to play it cool. Cool? Yeah, right. She was burning hotter than her favorite jalapeño poppers. Totally unacceptable. Caitlin smoothed a trembling hand across her stomach. "I think it's time to go home."

The fire in his eyes sparked brighter. "Good idea."

He'd misunderstood her, but she didn't correct him. Not when she now knew how good it felt to have his body pressed against hers. Not when she could easily imagine how good the contact would feel minus clothes. So easily.

She stilled when his hand brushed her cheek, the gentle touch sending another shiver through her. Her eyes flew to his. Was he going to kiss her again?

"The car's here," he said simply.

Other than the directions she gave him, they didn't speak on the way to her place. What was there to say? She knew what *he wanted. She knew what she wanted. She didn't know if she'd give in to her baser instincts. The last time she'd done something so reckless, it had cost her dearly.* But isn't nine years a long time to punish yourself? *a seductive inner voice whispered. Shouldn't she try to grab some fun with the sexiest man she'd ever laid eyes on when she had the chance? It didn't have to mean anything.*

"What do we do now?" *he asked outside her apartment. Resting his hand against the door, he crowded in. Damn, he smelled good. Looked even better. Kissed even better than that. All her favorite sins wrapped in one glorious package.*

What did they do now? There was only one acceptable answer. Heady desire thrumming through her veins, Caitlin rose on her toes and whispered in his ear. "We go inside and finish what we started."

Chirp, chirp!

Caitlin shot up straight in her bed, slapping a hand over her pounding heart. Unfortunately, her heart was no longer racing because of the best, steamiest dream she'd had in months. Hell, years.

Chirp, chirp!

She glared at the phone on her nightstand. A few months ago, she'd thought it would be funny to make singing birds her alarm clock ringtone. But if the birds didn't stop soon, she was going to reach inside the phone and wring their nonexistent necks. She silenced the phone mid-chirp, then flopped back on the bed.

Why was her subconscious betraying her by conjuring up something that hadn't happened? Other than cajoling her to take his phone number in case she changed her mind about helping him out for a longer period of time—"Hey, you never know," he'd said—Brady had been the perfect gentleman last night, walking her to her door and leaving her there with no propositions or kissing or touching. And she was okay with that. Ecstatic. Besides, it wasn't like she was ever going to see him again. Which was the way she wanted it to be. He was a complication she did not need. So her subconscious could suck it. She sat up again and after a decisive nod, got out of the bed.

An hour and a half later, she sat in her office at WTLK, where she worked as a radio show producer, Brady the last thing on her mind. She stabbed at the button to disconnect the conference call and made a face at Noelle.

"What are we going to do?" Noelle asked. "Ugh. I can't believe he dropped out."

"It wasn't good for his brand. Yeah, okay." She shook her head in annoyance. Noelle's radio talk show, *Noelle Knows*, was about to go into syndication, and Caitlin had locked down the perfect guest, Peter Carey, for the launch of the show. Or so she'd thought until five minutes ago when she'd received a phone call from his manager.

Noelle rolled her eyes. "He's a celebrity chef. How was doing the show going to harm him?"

"Radio is beneath him, didn't you hear? Never mind that people, you know the same people who go to his restaurants and spend money, listen to the radio. Dumbo." Caitlin did not like having her plans thwarted. She'd done a lot of research, narrowing down the candidate pool and then settling on Chef Boy. Obviously a mistake. There wasn't much time to find a replacement, but she would. She waved her hand. "Forget about him. I'll look through my contacts again. I'll find somebody. Somebody better."

"I'll look, too," Noelle said.

"Okay, but it's my job to procure talent, and I will." Going into syndication was the biggest professional challenge of her career, and she wanted to conquer it more than she'd wanted anything else in a long while. This was her chance to prove, once and for all, that she'd finally left old mistakes behind.

"I know you will, too, but remember, we're in this together." Noelle's lips pressed together in worry.

Frankly, Caitlin was worried, too. This close to launch date… This was her fault. She should've had a backup plan in place. It was part of a producer's job—anticipating all the curveballs thrown her way and hitting them out of the park. But she'd figure it out. She always did. "I've got this, and before you drive yourself crazy thinking about this *minor* setback, let's talk about something else."

Noelle's anxious expression didn't abate. "Like what?"

A logical question, except she hadn't gotten that far yet. "Umm, got any juicy gossip to share?"

To Caitlin's surprise, a sly look spread across Noelle's face. "As a matter of fact I do. Very juicy." She hesitated. "You might think otherwise."

"Why?" Caitlin asked, studying her friend.

Noelle leaned forward. "I suggest you go to the society page on the *Dallas Times* website, but while you do that, I'll tell you what you'll find. Something about Brady Hudson having a new lady friend and a photo of someone who looked remarkably like you kissing the daylights out of him."

"What?" Caitlin's fingers flew across the keyboard. When the website loaded, she stared at the screen in horror. "Oh God."

The kiss she'd initiated in order to convince Elise to back off had been captured for posterity. Their mouths were fused together. Brady's hands possessively cupped her butt, while her body was plastered against his. She clutched his shoulders like he was her anchor in the storm of lust. The most amazing kiss of her life.

"So you have a boyfriend," Noelle said, interrupting her trip down sensual memory lane. "Not that I heard that from you, of course, but I'm sure that's asking too much. After all, who tells their best friend they have a new boy toy? That went out with the Stone Ages."

Caitlin laughed, a welcome temporary distraction from the mortification sweeping through her body. She was thankful every day that she and Noelle had grown as close as sisters over the past year and a half while working on the show together. "I detect some sarcasm."

"Sarcasm yes, hurt no. Okay, I'll admit after the shock came the hurt for a second. But only a second. Wanna know why? Because my common sense returned. There is no way you'd be getting down and dirty with him without telling your best friend. I mean look at him."

"Hey! You have your own man."

A besotted smile spread across Noelle's face. "I do, and what a man he is. Tate is everything I could want and more." She held up a hand. "Be that as it may, that doesn't mean I can't appreciate another fine example of the male species."

"Hmmph." Caitlin returned her gaze to the computer. Not her first choice to have the kiss spread across the blogosphere. Or her second or third. Still, no need to panic. She hoped. People, even famous people like Brady, kissed all the time, and really, no one cared about her. And they hadn't used her last name. The article was mostly about Brady and how he hadn't wasted any time becoming familiar with Dallas women. She was only a placeholder, barely acknowledged, while they talked about him. Good. Maybe the story wouldn't hit the national gossip sites. Maybe. That would be her own personal nightmare.

Oh God. Blood froze in her veins. What if her mother found out? Caitlin drew in a breath. No, her mother wasn't interested in celebrity news, so hopefully she wouldn't see the story. Hopefully.

"We've gotten off topic," Noelle said. "Why don't you tell me what's going on, so I can feel superior in my deductive reasoning skills?" She fixed her I'm-a-psychologist-and-you-can-tell-me-anything look on Caitlin.

Caitlin sighed. Not that she hadn't planned on telling Noelle the truth, she just hadn't expected the news to travel so fast and wide. She stood and circled the desk to sit next to her friend. After glancing at the door to make sure it was 100 percent closed, she said, "Where do I start?"

"The beginning is usually a good place."

"Thank you, smart-ass."

Noelle preened. "I try."

Caitlin chuckled, then straightened her shoulders. "Here's the deal. You're right. Brady and I had never met until last night."

Her friend leaned toward her, her gray eyes gleaming. "What happened last night?"

Caitlin hesitated. She couldn't tell Noelle the real reason she'd gone to the Stampede event—to meet the biological father who'd left her mother and moved on to incredible success while her mom had been left to raise two kids on her own. Her BFF was a therapist and would start talking about healing. She didn't need to heal. She needed revenge. "I was on my way to the Stampede charity event when my car broke down."

Noelle's eyebrows arched. "You mean the car you should've had looked at six months ago?"

She sighed. "Yes." She continued the story, telling Noelle all about the evening, from Brady stopping to assist her to him asking her to help him fend off the team owner's daughter. "I agreed to the ruse since he'd helped me out."

"And y'all ended up engaging in a little exhibitionism."

"You know you can get out of my office at any time, right?"

Noelle snickered. "Sorry. Please continue."

"Anyway, she wasn't put off by my presence. I thought if she saw us kissing, she'd get the message. I didn't realize someone was out there playing paparazzi."

"So you aren't getting down and dirty with him?"

Caitlin laughed at the genuinely disappointed look on her best friend's face. "No, I just did him a favor. There will be no more kissing. If anyone asks, he can say we broke up or something."

"Well, that's no fun." Noelle peeked at her watch. "I guess gossip time is over. Back to the real world, i.e. going over my notes for the show."

After Noelle left, Caitlin returned to her desk to finish her own preparations. When she moved the mouse to wake up her computer, her eyes fell on the *Dallas Times* site again. She blinked. Below the story about her and Brady, there was another about the Stampede's head coach. Her father. Before she could think about it, she clicked the link, which led to a video that had aired on the local news.

"My wife and kids mean the world to me," Mack said. "I wouldn't be the man I am today or have accomplished all that I have without them." The camera shot widened to show Mack, his wife, and two kids posing for the perfect family portrait.

Fury tightened Caitlin's skin as memories swamped her. Her mother struggling to raise two small kids by herself. Struggling to make something of her own life. Doing so. She'd never complained, but Caitlin had heard her worrying about money and how she would juggle everything more than once over the years.

Her hand balled into a tight fist. Why had she lost her nerve last night? Brady or no Brady, she should have laid into the rat bastard. He deserved the whole speech she'd planned—right in front of all the journalists and cameras there to cover the event.

Her office phone rang. Her eyes still on the shot of Mack and his family, she picked it up. "Hello," she said absently.

"Caitlin Monroe?"

"Yes?"

"Hi, I'm Zach Brantley."

Caitlin dropped her head into her hand. Could her day get any worse?

Zach Brantley fancied himself as Dallas' own Harvey Levin, TMZ's founder. His website, zachsfacts.com, reported all the latest gossip about Dallas celebrities and made the *Dallas Times* society page look like child's play.

"How can I help you, Zach?" Her tone was as dry as a bone.

Not that Zach seemed to notice or care. His voice came out bright and chipper. "Word on the street is that you were running around last night telling everyone you were Brady Hudson's girlfriend. If I'd known that, I would have attended. Usually, those events are so boring. But not that photo! Hot stuff. Of course, those rank amateurs didn't catch your full name, but I am a pro and know everyone there is to know in Dallas, so I recognized you right off. Do you have a response?"

She made a murmuring sound, neither confirming nor denying his assertion. She would not panic.

"You're going to have to do better than that if you don't want me to publish my version of events."

She rolled her eyes at the phone before bringing it back to her ear. "Give me a break. You're going to publish it whether I comment or not." Much to her chagrin.

"True, but the story would be so much better if you gave me a quote."

Her gaze again landed on her computer, where Mack stared back at her with his perfect smile. All those times when she'd wanted braces, wanted to go to a summer camp that cost a little too much, but had never had the courage to ask for them, flashed through her mind. Her mom somehow knowing anyway and finding a way. She'd known her mother was amazing, but after finding that letter in her mom's closet last weekend when she'd been gathering clothes to donate to Goodwill, amazing seemed like such an inadequate word. An idea buzzed in her head. "Go ahead and publish your story if you want, but I have a much juicier one. If you're interested."

"You know I am," Zach replied, his giddiness practically reaching through the phone.

"I'll write an exclusive story for your site." She'd failed to get the retribution her mother deserved at casino night. She wouldn't fail again. To bring an asshole who'd conned everyone down—it would be glorious. And so well-deserved. And Mack and his misdeeds would be the focus, not her.

"Ooh, what about?"

"I can't tell you yet." Not till she'd gained some more info on dear old Dad to make the story especially explosive. To learn firsthand what a jerk he was. To get him to admit to what he'd done. Like abandoning his pregnant girlfriend with a stupid letter when he was about to turn pro because he didn't want any "distractions." Thinking a check for $5,000 would be enough to justify his actions. Never once mentioning that the kids he acknowledged weren't his firstborn. And she knew the perfect way to make that happen.

The shot clock let out a strident honk. The screeching of sneakers and the bouncing of basketballs came to an abrupt halt. Practice was over. Thank God.

His chest heaving, Brady bent at the waist, grabbed the bottom of his shorts, and sucked in desperately needed air. He'd pushed himself hard today. His teammates, too. Losing wasn't acceptable. Never would be. They *would* win their game tonight. They'd worked hard today. Harder than they usually did during a game-day, walk-through practice, but he was okay with it. Last night had been a much-needed reprieve. But it was time to get back to the grind. To remember why they were all there. To come together to win a championship.

You played hero ball.

The accusation played through his mind for the millionth time since Caitlin, all five-two of her, had offered her opinion. Is that what he'd done? He trusted himself above all others. He'd seen a sliver of a path to the basket and taken it. Until the referee blew the whistle and assessed him a foul. Bullshit.

He was Brady Hudson.

It sounded conceited, and, okay, yes it was conceited, but it was also the truth. Everybody knew there was a star system in the NBA and the best players got favorable calls. It had been a close play, and he should've been given the benefit of the doubt.

That's not how the referee saw it. You had a guy open in the corner.

More unsolicited wisdom from his outspoken pretend girlfriend. Brady sighed. Was she right? He'd told himself he was helping his team, doing what it took to win, but had he let his ego get in the way of a win?

A whistle blew, cutting through the endless loop of his going-nowhere thoughts. At least practice had been closed to the media. He didn't want to answer any more questions about the game or his less-than-enthusiastic postgame comments that had ended up as the lead story on SportsCenter, the anchors shaking their heads at his bad attitude, wondering if his stint in Dallas would be over before it started.

The players came together in groups of two or three. Mack handed his ever-present clipboard to Frank, one of the assistant coaches, and clapped his hands together. "Good practice. I liked the hustle I saw today. Our zone defense needs some work, but it's getting there." He swept his all-seeing gaze down the line, stopping to rest on each player for a second—more than a few seconds on Brady. Was Coach going to mention the last play of the game? Brady met his eyes directly. He wasn't afraid. He couldn't be afraid.

His teammates were watching.

Mack continued down the line, and then nodded as though satisfied with what he saw in his players' faces. "That's it for now. See you tonight."

Brady joined his teammates trudging off the court toward the locker room.

"Hudson." Coach.

Brady stopped and let the others pass, ignoring their curious looks. Especially the ones filled with barely concealed glee.

When the double doors slammed behind the players, assistant coaches, and trainers, Brady grabbed a towel from a rack at the edge of the court and wiped the sweat from his brow. "What's up?"

Coach braced his legs apart and crossed his arms across a wide chest. He'd retired from the league fifteen years ago, but he still had the build of an active player. A white polo with the team's logo on the right breast tucked into black warmup pants attested to that. "I gave you time to cool off and let you have fun last night."

Brady's grip on the towel tightened. "But?"

"About that play last game."

Brady had expected to be summoned into Mack's office immediately after the game, once the media had filed out of the locker room. He wondered what had taken Mack so long.

"Yes?" he said, pleased his voice came out steady. Mack was six-six, which meant Brady had to look up to him, but he did so without reservation. He respected his coach, but he wouldn't cower. Not even when he suspected his eardrums would be ringing in a few seconds from all the yelling.

Mack sighed. "I understand what you were trying to do. I

appreciate the competitive fire. But you have four teammates with you on the court. You don't have to take it all on your shoulders. All you need to do to succeed here is keep your nose clean and play basketball."

He wasn't going to get his ass handed to him? Really? He'd take it. "Got it." Brady used the excuse of wiping his face with the towel to exhale in relative privacy.

"Oh, but Hudson?"

He glanced up. And met Mack's scorching glower.

"If you ever pull that shit again, your ass is mine. Believe that."

Brady did. Mack had a completely deserved reputation as a hard-ass. A fair and intelligent hard-ass who'd forgotten more about the game of basketball than Brady could ever hope to know, but a hard-ass all the same. Brady nodded once and left the practice gym.

Most of his teammates had taken advantage of their head start on him and were already in the shower. He made his way to his locker and stared at the nameplate on the top shelf, his name etched in the Stampede's signature purple. At times, he still found it hard to believe he no longer wore the Knicks' blue and orange.

He was an arrogant son of a bitch. He knew that. Had never seen any problem with it. The NBA was a business. And the best way to succeed in business was to show up every day ready to work as hard as you could. And he'd done that. He was the best point guard in the league. That wasn't up for debate. He had the records, the accolades, the awards to prove it.

Yes, he was the best. He demanded the best from his teammates. The other players could either get with the program or get the hell out. They respected him, even if they didn't necessarily like him, something that had never bothered him much.

Until the day he'd been told to get out. Because the team had stopped winning. And he'd made a perfect scapegoat. Especially after the punch heard 'round the world happened.

He'd found himself in his coach's office facing the Knicks' general manager, Jesse Waters. Waters didn't like him because Brady had been there before him. He hated that when Brady spoke, people listened. That Brady's opinion mattered to everyone in the organization. That important team decisions weren't made until Brady was consulted.

"You've become a disrupting influence in the locker room," Waters said, leaning back in his chair, shaking his head, his disappointment cloying in its fakeness.

Brady gripped the chair arms hard until the leather bit into his palms to stop himself from leaping up and strangling Waters. He couldn't stand the sanctimonious prick. "Are you fucking kidding me? *I'm* the disrupting influence?"

"Yes. When you demand another player be traded, you're disrupting."

"Because Jenkins doesn't know the meaning of loyalty. Of what it means to be a team guy."

"Neither do you. You want to get rid of a guy with his skillset because he slept with your girlfriend, who you shouldn't have been dating anyway. Team rules about not fraternizing with dancers and other employees weren't enforced because no one wanted to upset the great Brady Hudson, and look what happened. It's time for a change if we're going to go to the next level."

Brady spoke through gritted teeth. "I'll take the team to the next level."

"Hudson, come on." Oiliness oozed in the words. "We haven't been to the Finals in three years. The past few years, we've been knocked out earlier and earlier in the playoffs. Last year, we didn't come close to making it. And our record so far this season, well, I don't have to tell you what that is."

"Maybe if you did your job and knew how to evaluate talent, we wouldn't be in this mess," Brady shot back.

The GM's blue eyes flashed. "I can evaluate talent just fine. Your talent isn't where it used to be. Deandre Baker is ready to step in as the starting point guard. You have no one to blame but yourself. Fighting with a teammate over a woman."

"I already told you what happened."

"Did you or did you not punch Jenkins in the locker room, which turned into the top story on SportsCenter?"

Brady wouldn't defend himself. It didn't matter. Waters' mind was already made up. It didn't matter that Brady's skills hadn't eroded. Waters had his new pet in Baker and couldn't wait to exert his authority over the team once Brady was gone. He didn't bother glancing at his coach, Ted Carson. Carson wouldn't be much help. Not when he was concerned about holding on to his own job. Nothing shocking there. Number one rule of the NBA. Of life. People looked out for themselves first. Always. He'd learned that lesson over and over throughout his thirty years on Earth.

Brady had left the meeting and headed back to the locker room. He'd expected some backing from his teammates, guys he'd known and played with for years. He didn't receive it. Oh, they'd paid lip service about being sad to see him go, but he wasn't born yesterday. He thought if anyone would see past the bullshit, it would be his teammates. That they were coworkers and not bosom buddies had never bothered him, but no one had reached out to him. No one had stood up for him.

Now he was a member of the Dallas Stampede. The first time in eleven years he'd been the new guy in the locker room. His new teammates had heard the rumors. That he'd used the girlfriend thing as an excuse to get Jenkins traded. That he really wanted Jenkins gone because he was usurping Brady's role as the best player on the team. That he'd divided the locker room. That he was a me-guy who put himself above the team. All bullshit. Pride had kept him from defending himself.

Brady dropped onto the bench in front of the locker and unlaced his high tops. He eased the shoes off and flexed his feet.

He simply wanted to win. Push everybody to be the best they could be. The only way he knew how to do that was with his play on the court. So he needed to get better. He would get better. There was no other choice.

With a resolute nod, he stood, stretched his back, and headed to the shower. Half an hour later, he exited the locker room and headed for the garage.

"Hey, Brady, hold up!"

He halted while the "fucks" started taking round-trip flights through his head.

Elise hurried up to him, breathless. "Hey."

"Hey," he answered with a forced smile.

"How was practice?"

"Intense."

"Well, that should pay off tonight. The Jazz are on a three-game losing streak." She stepped directly in front of him, clearly not giving a damn about personal space, and stroked his arm.

And of course, Maguire chose that moment to walk by. He didn't stop, but he did shoot a disgusted look over his shoulder before he opened the door leading to the garage. Fuck.

Shifting his attention back to Elise, Brady shrugged and stepped back. "Maybe. Can't take anyone for granted though."

"Is your girlfriend going to be there tonight?"

His cell phone rang, offering the perfect excuse not to answer her. Even more so when he saw who was calling. "Sorry. I have to take this." He stepped a few feet away, well aware that Elise was listening.

"Hey, sweetheart," he said to Caitlin.

"Let me guess," she said drily. "Elise is there."

"Got it in one." He continued toward the exit. Thankfully, Elise headed in the opposite direction toward the team offices. When he was sure she was out of hearing range, he continued, "Ms. Caitlin. Couldn't stop thinking about me?"

"Hardly." The sniff was silent, but loud nonetheless.

A smile broke across his face. She was fun. And if he thought about her and the kiss that had ended their night, well, it was only because it had been so unexpected. And okay, he wondered if it had been as spectacular as his memory insisted it was. "How can I believe you when you called me less than twenty-four hours after we parted ways?"

"It'll be hard for you I know, but put your pretty little head to the task and try."

"You think I'm pretty?"

"I insult you and that's what you choose to concentrate on?"

"That's because I know you didn't mean it."

Grumbling emitted through the phone. Brady struggled not to laugh. This was exactly what he needed after a hard practice.

"We need to talk. In person."

He stopped walking. She didn't sound upset. A little nervous, maybe. "Okay. Where do you suggest?"

"My job. I can't leave, but I want to get this taken care of ASAP."

Surprise darted through him. He hadn't expected that, but she'd hooked him. "Give me the address."

Ten minutes later, he arrived at the building that housed the radio station WTLK. The woman at the front desk buzzed Caitlin, who came sashaying down the hall a minute later. She looked good. Not as dressed up as the previous night, obviously, but good. Great actually. The green of the sweater complemented the sienna tone of her skin and clung to pert breasts. Before meeting Caitlin, if anyone had asked him, he would have said the bigger, the better, but now… His gaze traveled up past plump lips, a small nose that was the definition of cute, to her big doe eyes.

"Brady, hi. Please follow me." Her hips gently swung side to side as she led him to her office and shut the door behind him. "Is the fake girlfriend gig still open?" she asked with no preamble.

"Absolutely."

She nodded. "Great. I want in."

Just like that? Yeah, there was more to the story than her wanting to help him out. He crossed his arms over his chest. "Tell me what's going on."

"You need a favor." Her chin lifted. "And I need a favor."

Now they were getting somewhere. "What kind of favor?"

"I produce a radio show that's about to go into syndication. To kick it off, we need a guest with a name."

"Let me guess. I'm the name."

"Yes." She beamed a call-me-a-genius smile.

He wasn't ready to acquiesce. Not yet. "What kind of show?"

"Relationship advice."

He suppressed a groan. Really? What the hell did he know about relationships? "What would I be doing?"

"Ideally, you'll come into the studio, but we can do it over the phone if need be. We'll do a Love Letters to Brady segment where you offer advice to callers. The host, Noelle, will probably tell you you're wrong, but the listeners will love it."

"That's it?"

"Yep. It will be one day out of your life. You should do it." She sounded certain. Too certain.

"Why?"

"It'll give you a chance to get away from the game for a bit."

"I don't want to get away from the game."

Caitlin clasped her hands together. "Okay, look. How do I say this? You have a reputation for being difficult and arrogant."

"I am." He shrugged.

She shot him a look. "Be that as it may, underneath all the arrogance, you're a good guy."

Brady shifted, uncomfortable with the label. He'd looked out for himself for so long, relying solely on himself, trusting no one because doing so always blew up in his face, that he'd stopped thinking of himself as a good guy a long time ago.

"Doing the show will present you in a new, less intense light to all the naysayers."

Which sounded good except he didn't give a shit about his reputation. But he needed to, if he was being honest with himself. If the media heard him giving advice to others and acting like a regular guy, maybe they would back off and stop crowding around his locker looking for quotes that painted him in a bad light. Maybe his teammates would stop thinking of him as a raging egotist, only out for himself.

"If that doesn't convince you, need I remind you that you need a pretend girlfriend?" Caitlin drove home the point he couldn't ignore even if he wanted to.

Yes, he needed a girlfriend, especially after the scene Maguire witnessed.

He focused in on the mastermind of this plot. "So if I do what you want, you'll do what I want. How real would this pretend relationship be? Ms. Caitlin, are you trying to get in my pants?"

Her eyes widened. "No. I'm not sleeping with you."

"I don't recall asking you to." Her glare only made him

grin harder. "I just wanted to see where your head was at."

"I'm not interested in you. This is strictly a business proposition." She ticked her fingers. "No sleeping together. No kissing other than polite kisses on the cheek when the situation calls for it. No touching. No—"

Brady held up a hand. "I get it." He refused to acknowledge the twinge of *something* that hit near his chest *again* at her assertion that she wasn't interested in him.

She stared up at him again with those pleading, beautiful eyes. "Will you do it?"

Brady studied her. Caitlin had been nothing but honest and straightforward with him, something he appreciated more than he could say. She didn't want to get involved with him. She'd made that abundantly clear. Good. His last girlfriend had taught him that he was much better off concentrating on basketball than letting someone who'd only end up hurting him get close. The story of his life. So, yes, he could and would hold Caitlin at arm's length. Just because he'd lain awake for half the night reliving their kiss didn't mean he couldn't control his hormones. As he'd proven over and over, he could accomplish whatever he put his mind to.

Besides, it was only a few weeks. Maybe not even that long. How bad could it be?

"Fine. I'm in." Despite Caitlin's claims, he wasn't a nice guy, but he was opportunistic. "You can start tonight. We have a game. I would love to have my *girlfriend* there cheering me on."

Chapter Four

"Thanks for coming with me," Caitlin said to her twin brother, Christian, as they maneuvered through the crowd milling in the arena concourse. She clutched a twelve-dollar margarita in her hand. Ordinarily she would have balked at the price, but she needed the liquid courage to get through the night.

Yes, she was being dramatic, and yes, this whole pretense had been her idea, but she hadn't given proper consideration to what attending Brady's games entailed. Like trying to pretend she didn't notice everyone in the arena staring at her.

At the moment, she was regretting her decision not to sit in the suite Brady had offered to get for her. Not that she wanted to sit in a suite. She preferred sitting in the stands with fellow loud and rowdy fans, but a suite would have been more private. Way fewer eyeballs on her. But wasn't that the point? Eyeballs on her while she played the dutiful girlfriend? So she needed to get it together. The margarita would help.

"No problem," Christian said. "How could I say no to free tickets to a Stampede game *and* a chance to check out my sister's new boyfriend?"

"Shut up, Chris," she said mildly. Her brother had that quiet sarcasm thing down cold. She'd told him she was "dating" Brady in exchange for him being a guest on the radio show because he knew she'd never date an athlete in a million years. Not after her football player ex played her for the biggest fool known to mankind. Christian didn't know about their *fa*—Mack— yet. She wanted to get his impressions of the coach before laying that news on him. Christian was the epitome of calm. But she had a feeling her news would ruffle even his normally unruffleable feathers. He'd never talked about their father growing up—even when she wondered who he was, Christian was always the one to shrug off her curiosity, saying he didn't know and didn't care.

And maybe you haven't told him because you don't want him to tell you that your plan is stupid. That maybe you shouldn't be involving an innocent party in your scheme.

A thought that had occurred to her with startling frequency since she'd come up with this idea. But she couldn't stop now. Pretending to date Brady was the easiest, most natural way to gain access to Mack to get some dirt on him. Brady wouldn't get hurt. When everything came to light, she'd make sure everyone understood that he'd known nothing about her plot.

"What?" Christian asked, breaking into her thoughts. "I asked a perfectly innocent question."

She side-eyed him. "Yeah, okay."

Caitlin sidestepped a woman who'd abruptly stopped in the middle of the concourse, all without spilling a drop of her margarita. There was a God. "Has Mama said anything about the photo?"

He shook his head. "No."

"Good. Maybe that means she hasn't seen it."

"Maybe." Or she was waiting to strike with a well-planned attack, his expression said. Miranda Monroe never acted without thinking it all the way through first and then double-thinking just in case.

They entered the arena bowl and climbed the stairs to their seats. Again, eyes latched on to her while she and Christian completed the excuse-me shuffle step to their seats in the middle of the row. She did her best to ignore them and the tension creeping into her shoulders, but couldn't stop a sigh of relief from escaping when she reached her seat with no drink or ass spillage.

She took a sip of her margarita. No one spoke to her. So awkward. And ridiculous. Time to take matters into her own hands.

"Hi, I'm Caitlin Monroe," she said to an older lady sitting a few seats away, who wore a bedazzled number 43 jersey. Dante Whitmore's number.

The woman took her laser-like focus off the court where the players were warming up long enough to look Caitlin up and down. "Honey, I know who you are. Thanks to that kiss, everyone in this arena knows who you are."

Great.

She'd met a few of the wives and girlfriends at casino night. They'd been nice enough, but she'd sensed their reticence. They weren't sure what to make of her. How would she change the group dynamics? Would she bring drama? Would she be a permanent fixture or a one-and-doner? Caitlin's lips lifted in a slight smile. "That kiss is not what I expected my claim to fame to be."

"Don't worry about it," a woman said from behind her. "It was hot!" She held out her hand. "I'm Michelle Banks, by the way. We met at casino night. Victor Banks is my husband."

"I remember. It's nice to see you again." Caitlin shook Michelle's hand. Michelle looked to be about Caitlin's age. Pretty with shoulder-length black hair. Victor Banks was a backup forward on the team. He'd been a member of the team for the past two years, if she remembered correctly. Solid performer. Nothing fancy, but he could be counted on to grab a few rebounds and be at the right spot at the right time on the court.

Michelle tapped the shoulder of the older woman. "This is Stacy Whitmore, Dante Whitmore's mother."

"I come to every game," Stacy said proudly. She peered around Caitlin's shoulder. "Who's that? Surely you're not bold enough to bring a date to your boyfriend's game."

Caitlin laughed. "No, this is my brother Christian."

He waved. "Nice to meet you, ladies."

"Oh, it's our pleasure, believe me," Stacy said. "I might be old enough to be your mother, but I can still appreciate a fine man. Don't worry. I don't bite. Too hard."

Christian tilted his cup toward her in acknowledgment. "Good to know."

"You're cute, honey. You look like someone. Can't put my finger on who though."

Caitlin stilled. She'd always wondered how Christian had managed to top six feet when she and their mother were so petite. Mack had four or five inches on him and was probably thirty or forty pounds heavier, but now that she knew about their relationship, it was easy to see Mack in Christian in the curve of his jaw and shape of his nose.

"You think so?" Christian said. "Maybe I'm the man of your dreams?"

Caitlin snorted and smacked him on the arm. "Calm down, Romeo."

"Now that we've got the niceties out of the way, let's get to the good stuff," Michelle said. "How did you meet Brady?"

Stacy tapped Caitlin on the leg. "No, let's be really real. Tell us what a great kisser he is. With lots and lots of detail."

Caitlin sensed no malice in their questions, only run-of-the-mill nosiness. If the situation were reversed, she'd be just as curious. "Okay, here's the deal." She leaned closer to Michelle. "Brady is…a great kisser. And that's all you're going to get out of me."

Stacy joined Michelle in booing.

Caitlin laughed.

"I like you," Michelle said. "You know how to have fun. Guess that explains why he doesn't hang out with the guys."

Caitlin worked to keep the surprise off her face. Brady *never* hung out with his new teammates? Is that why he and Maguire were at each other's throats at the casino night?

"Oh, hush," Stacy said. "Sounds romantic to me."

"Let me tell you this in case you don't know, but that was the hottest kiss I've seen in a long time," Michelle said.

Caitlin struggled not to fidget. The kiss had been devastating. An impulse on her part that had landed her in an untenable situation, but she still couldn't muster any regret for her actions. It had been spectacular. Never to be repeated again, but amazing all the same. When she did find someone suitable to date, the bar had been raised, oh, about twenty stories.

A new voice joined the conversation. "I heard Hudson was about to get engaged to his girlfriend in New York."

Caitlin twisted her body toward the aisle where a stunning woman in five-inch gold heels, skinny jeans, and the best weave Caitlin had ever seen stood with a smirk on her expertly made-up face. Behind her stood two more women cut from the same mold.

Girlfriend? Engaged? The struggle was real to keep the shock off her face this time. She could only hope she'd succeeded. It was the surprise of the announcement, not the thought that he'd almost belonged to someone else that sent her heart racing, of course.

"Don't you think it's too early to start with the silliness,

Patrice?" Michelle asked, her tone impatient. "The game hasn't even started."

Patrice and her mini-mes swanned into the empty seats next to Caitlin. Lord, why hadn't she agreed to sit in a suite? Because she'd thought she'd get more bang for her buck if she was out here. If she had one more big, bright idea, she was going to figure out a way to kick herself in the shin.

Patrice pasted a bright smile on her face. "I'm sorry. I wasn't trying to cause trouble. I assumed the love of Hudson's life would know all about his past. I mean you wouldn't want to be his rebound, would you?" Her lips pouted in the saddest attempt at an empathetic look Caitlin had ever seen in her life.

Puh-lease.

"Of course not," Caitlin said brightly, her composure regained. "Brady and I share everything, which is why I know about his girlfriend—excuse me, *ex*-girlfriend—in New York. You say he was about to propose. Well, he didn't, and that's all that matters."

"If you say so."

"I do." Caitlin tilted her head to the side. "I'm sorry. Who are you again?"

"I'm Patrice Houston. Soon to be *Maguire*." She waved her left hand, showing off a blinding rock.

Oh, great. Lance Maguire's other half. Explained the attitude. No telling what Lance had been saying about Brady to her. "Nice to meet you," she said as politely as she could.

The bright lights in the arena shut off and were replaced by the sequence of flashing spotlights used to introduce the starting lineup. Loud, thumping music filled the air. A video of the players urging the crowd to stand and get loud played on the Jumbotron.

"From USC, in his eleventh year, Brady Hudson!" the public address announcer yelled.

The crowd roared. He walked down the line the bench players formed, high-fiving his teammates. As befitting her role as fake girlfriend, Caitlin screamed along with the crowd. As the most tenured player on the team and the Stampede's annual All-Star, Lance Maguire was the last player introduced. He played to the crowd, cupping his ear to get them to scream louder.

The game started a few minutes later. Caitlin was immediately drawn into the action. "Come on, ref! That wasn't a block," she yelled when Brady was called for a foul.

Michelle looked at her with respect. "You know your stuff. I see why Brady likes you even if…"

"Even if what?"

Michelle glanced around, clearly checking to make sure no one was paying them any attention. She leaned in. "Even if I'm kind of surprised that Brady got involved so quickly. Oh, not because of you. Based on what my husband and a few of the other players say, he's so aloof. The guys aren't sure what his deal is. Is he riding the year out to get to free agency and get a contract? Only interested in padding his stats?"

Caitlin took a sip of her drink to give herself a moment to gather her thoughts. "I don't know why he's acting that way." And wasn't that the truth? How well did she really know Brady? "All I can say is that's not the person I know. He's warm and funny. I can say that he cares. A lot. And not about padding his stats. He was devastated about the loss the other night. The part he played in it. He wants the team to win and to get better. He's dedicated himself to that."

Michelle nodded. "Everyone thought they'd have a better record at this point than they do. It's early in the season, but winning at the five-hundred level isn't going to get them into the playoffs let alone win a championship. Plus, when Brady was traded here, it threw a lot of guys off. Got them wondering if they were next on the chopping block. Fun times in Stampedeland, let me tell you."

Caitlin grimaced. "Sounds like it."

She turned her attention back to the court in time to see Brady steal the ball from the opposing point guard, outrun two defenders chasing him down the court, and slam the ball through the hoop. She leaped out of her seat and pumped her fist. "Yeah!"

She watched the rest of the game, enthralled. It was clear Brady was on a mission. Determined to make up for his mistake from the last game, maybe? Whatever the case, he was everywhere at once. She almost pitied his opponents. The crowd gasped as one when he made an incredible low, bouncing pass between two Jazz players, who never saw it coming. Tilly caught the ball underneath the basket and dunked it home, sending the Stampede fans into rapturous cheers.

After the game, at Michelle's urging, she and Christian went down into the tunnel to wait for Brady. "All the wives do it," Michelle said. "We can't go into the locker room, but we can wait until they come out. They'll be in a good mood."

The Stampede had ended their two-game losing streak, blowing out the Jazz 100-84.

"Your man, especially," Michelle added.

Brady had scored twenty-three points and dished out eleven assists, playing one of his best games as a member of the Stampede.

But *her* man? No, he wasn't. And that was as it should be.

The corridor was packed with game officials and everyone else biding their time until the players came out. After Michelle excused herself to take a phone call, Caitlin settled against the wall next to Christian to wait. With showers, media interviews, and whatever else players did after a game, it might be a while.

"Ms. Monroe, I was hoping to see you tonight!" Dale

Templeton came striding down the hall, beaming.

Curious gazes swung between her and the exuberant team owner, but she wouldn't wilt underneath the scrutiny. She'd gotten herself into this mess, after all. "Hi, Mr. Templeton," she said with a smile. "It's nice to see you again."

"I can see why you and Brady get along. Both stubborn and refuse to call me by the name I told you to." He enveloped her in a hug, surprising the crap out of her. She went along for the ride because, well, she didn't have any other choice. The scents of some piney cologne and expensive silk filled her nose. She met the suspicious eyes of his daughter over his shoulder.

He stepped back and grinned at her. "How long have you been waiting?"

"Not long."

"Too long. A man should never let a beautiful woman wait."

Since Caitlin didn't think Brady had any idea she was out here, she wasn't sure how to respond. "Thanks, but I'm okay."

"Give me a second. I have something I want to discuss with both of you."

He did? "Uh…"

But he was already gone, slipping inside the locker room, leaving her alone with Elise, who was openly eyeing her and Christian. Great. She forced herself to smile. "Elise, this is my brother, Christian."

"Hello," she said in that cool voice of hers.

"Nice to meet you," Christian returned politely.

"You, too." Her phone rang. "Excuse me. I have to take this." She put the phone to her ear and strode away. Christian turned to Caitlin, his eyebrows raised. She shrugged.

The door to the locker room swung open. Dale clapped his hands. "Everyone, can you join us inside? The players are decent."

Caitlin wasn't sure she wanted to go into the inner sanctum of the locker room. She sure as hell didn't belong there. But left with no choice, she filed in with the other family members, friends, and team employees.

Along with the players, the room was filled with reporters and a few cameramen from the local news channels. In the middle of the carpeted floor, a circular Stampede logo dominated. She zeroed in on her pretend boyfriend, who was indeed dressed. The thought of Brady Hudson with only a towel wrapped around his waist to protect his modesty threatened to warp all her brain cells. Good thing she hadn't walked in on that. She would've slipped in a puddle of drool. Not that the blue sweater he wore helped her predicament much. The wool contoured to his broad shoulders, wide chest, and biceps. The man was built.

His brow lifted in query. She smoothed her features the best she could. Lord only knew what he'd read on her face. Good old-fashioned lust, probably.

The other friends and family went to stand next to their loved ones, so she did the same. Christian, as was his way, hung back, to take in the scene. "Hey, Brady," she said. "Good game."

His lips lifted in a brief smile. "Thanks. Winning was the only option tonight."

"Yeah, I gathered that based on the way you played like a man possessed." She moved in closer and whispered, "Do you know what's going on?"

His large hand landed at the small of her back, sending a flash of heat radiating up her back. He leaned down, his breath caressing her ear, the sound of his deep voice sliding through her like melted chocolate. "Hey back. Not a clue."

They turned their attention to the middle of the room where Dale stood on the logo. Obviously used to being the center of attention, he practically preened. "As you all know, there is nothing I value more than family. I loved my wife with all my heart before she passed away. My daughter is an important part of the Stampede family, as are all of our employees from the ball boys to the general manager. That includes the players. A couple of weeks ago, we acquired the best point guard in the league. And because he quickly realized there is no woman quite like a Dallas woman, he scooped up Caitlin, who I've chatted with a few times. I'm a great judge of character and know Brady chose well."

All those eyes that had been trained on Dale were now centered directly on Caitlin and Brady. His hand tensed against her back. Where was Dale going with this? The sinking feeling in her stomach told her she wouldn't be thrilled when he was done with his speech.

Dale clasped his hands together, an entirely-too-pleased-with-himself gleam entering his eyes. "So what better way to welcome Brady and Caitlin to the Stampede family than by including them in the annual team cookbook? As you all know, it's my pet project. My restaurants and food were my passion before I bought the Stampede, and I love sharing that passion with our fans. Where's Nick? Nick is the team's official photographer," he said to Caitlin. "Oh, there he is." He called out the man's name and waved him over. The photographer carried an intimidating, professional-looking camera in his hand. "Now kiss Caitlin like you mean it, Brady. We need a shot for the cookbook. Nick's the best in the business. He can do better than some camera phone photo."

The urge to bolt slammed into her with the force of a tornado. Not that she could since she was finding the process of breathing to be almost beyond her abilities at the moment. Forget about actually moving. All those nightmares she had about being the center of attention? They were coming true at this very moment. She wasn't asleep. She was very much awake. And very much the center of attention. She estimated there were about seventy-five people in the room, which meant there were one hundred and fifty eyes on her.

Did Dale really expect them to reenact *Seven Minutes in Heaven* in the middle of this room? Judging by the expectant look on his face, the answer was a resounding yes.

Stiffly, her muscles protesting the entire way, she turned and looked up into the eyes of the man she'd dragged into this fiasco with her. Thankfully, she didn't detect imminent murder in his eyes. His face was blank. Not great, but better than murder, she supposed. He didn't speak, curling a strong arm around her waist and drawing her closer. He lowered his head. Her eyes fluttered closed as she rose on her toes to meet him halfway. The soft press of his sculpted mouth against hers didn't last long. A second at the most. It didn't matter. The riot of sensation that rampaged through her system attested to that. Her lips tingled, begging for more.

No. She stepped back out of his hold and forced her lips upward. "There you go, Mr. Templeton."

He harrumphed. "You call that a kiss? I know you can do better than that. We all do. We saw the picture."

Had she said this was getting out of control? Now *this* was getting out of control.

"You call that a kiss, Hudson? My dog gives better kisses than that," Victor called out.

"You need lessons, man? I'd be happy to step in with your lady and show you how it's done," Tilly taunted.

Brady glared. "Like hell." He hauled Caitlin against his chest and laid one on her. A full assault that bombarded all her senses. His hard body plastered against hers. The taste of him, slightly minty, the way he used his lips and tongue to entice, then demand a response from her enthralled her. Her hands landed on his arms, and she held on to enjoy the ride. His scent, so delicious, so Brady, wrapped around her. The kiss was thorough. Better than she remembered. She'd tried to tell herself that the kiss on the bench wasn't as great as she'd thought it was. She'd been right. It was better.

Loud cheers finally penetrated her consciousness. Slowly, Brady ended the embrace. By the skin of her teeth, she held back the whimper that threatened to spill from her lips. She gulped in oxygen. Brady's eyes were no longer blank. The hunger for more was easy for her to read. Especially because she felt the same way. Although the kiss was everything she could have wanted, she wanted more. Everything he had to offer. And that was the most dangerous thought of all. She shouldn't want more. Couldn't want more. It would end in disaster—especially since she was using this fake relationship to get closer to his coach.

Dale tapped her on the arm, giving her an excuse to turn away from the scorching look in Brady's eyes. "Now that's what I'm talking about."

"Show's over, Dale," someone called out, walking over to join them. Mack. How had she missed his presence? Probably because she'd been so caught up in Brady she hadn't thought to look for him when she'd entered the room. Not good. He was supposed to be her priority, not Brady. "I'm sure you got what you needed," Mack said to Nick.

The photographer tapped his camera. "Believe me, I did. Ten times over."

Mack scanned the room. "I'll see everyone tomorrow." In other words—dismissed. Someone called Mack's name, and he headed in that direction before she could gather her thoughts and talk to him.

Brady turned back to his locker. Awkwardness filled her pores. What was she supposed to do now? At least the other people in the room were returning to their own conversations and had stopped staring at them.

"I guess I'll see you later," she said to Brady's back. She moved to head back to Christian, who was observing everything in the corner with a wry smile and standing next to Elise, who did not have a smile on her face.

A strong hand landed on her arm, halting her progress. The electric spark that raced up her arm let her know who had stopped her.

"Where are you going?" Brady's face had once again turned expressionless, but his voice still worked wonders on her. His touch, too.

She turned, breaking his hold, immediately missing the connection. "Home."

"How did you get here?"

"I came with my brother. He drove."

"I'll take you home."

Twenty more minutes in a tiny space with Brady? She didn't think she, her hormones, or her senses could take that. "That's okay."

"No, it's not." He leaned in closer until there was definitely not enough space in between them. "How would it look if my girlfriend was seen leaving with someone else when I'm more than capable of taking you home? I can hear it now. Trouble in paradise."

Oh. Good point. Damn logic.

She went to relay the change of plans to her brother. Brady joined her soon thereafter. She made sure the introductions were short and sweet. No need to give Christian a chance to make any comments he'd no doubt think were hilarious. A minute later, she was headed out the locker room. With Brady at her side.

In the hall outside the locker room, they passed Lance Maguire, who took the opportunity to lean in and whisper, "Nice show. Dale's found the son he never had."

Brady, to his credit, never slowed.

The mood in his car could best be described as tense. She still hadn't recovered from the kiss. She felt off-kilter. Heart racing too fast. She'd felt way too much for someone she shouldn't. A kiss that was still rocking her world. Being next to him. Smelling him. Remembering how it felt to be in his arms. None of that was helping her state of mind. "Why did you kiss me like that?"

Brady's hands tightened on the steering wheel. "What was I supposed to do? I couldn't kiss you like my great aunt Bertha again, could I?"

"No, but it was still too much."

His eyes clashed with hers. "This whole charade is too much. This isn't what I signed up for."

"It's not what I signed up for either!"

"This arrangement was supposed to get the guys off my back so they didn't think I was trying to get in good with Dale by dating his daughter. Now he's making a big deal about it in the middle of the locker room in front of everybody."

Caitlin shook her head. "Now you're concerned about what they think?"

"What is that supposed to mean?" A thread of steel had entered his voice.

"Nothing. Forget I said anything."

"No. Speak your mind. Don't go shy now."

"Your teammates don't know what to think of you. Maybe you should open up to them."

"I've got this," he snapped. "We have to play better. We don't need to be bosom buddies off the court."

"Like Tom Hanks?"

He blinked. "What?"

"*Bosom Buddies*. You know, the eighties sitcom. He dressed up in drag so he could live in an all-women's apartment building."

"*Huh?*"

"It's true. My mom made me and my brother watch reruns when we were little. Look it up on YouTube. I wonder if it's on Netflix or Hulu? The premise sounds dumb I know."

A note of incredulity entered his voice. "Are we really talking about this now?"

"Better this than you biting my head off."

Brady pulled into a parking space at her place and turned off the car. He didn't make a move to get out of the car. Neither did she. He stared out the windshield for a few seconds, then turned to her. "I'm sorry. I'm under a lot of stress right now. I shouldn't take it out on you."

She saw the truth in his eyes. She longed to touch him, to offer comfort. But that wasn't her place. She didn't want it to be her place, right? Right. "Apology accepted. I'm sorry for lashing out at you."

"Apology accepted." He reached out to brush aside a strand of her hair, his eyes searching hers. "Where do we go from here?"

"Do you want to quit?" She held her breath.

Brady dropped his hand to his side. "No. This is still the best way to keep Elise at arm's length." A brief smile touched his lips. "The guys can't complain I'm after her after that public display."

The relief rushing through her was embarrassing in its intensity, but only because she needed Brady to gain access to Mack. That's all it was. "Okay."

"I know I've put you in some awkward positions, and you haven't bailed yet. Thank you. It means a lot."

The compliment surprised her. Warmed her. "You're welcome, but don't forget you're helping me, too. Thank you."

"You're welcome." His voice, so deep, so alluring, made her long for things she shouldn't.

She forced an upbeat tone in her voice. "Guess that settles it then. We'll keep on faking it."

His dark eyes pierced hers. "Yeah. Faking it."

Chapter Five

"You sure about this?" Noelle asked.

Caitlin didn't need to ask for clarification. "Yes, I'm sure." Mostly sure. No. One hundred percent sure. "Yes. Brady will be perfect." She ticked off points on her fingers. "He has an edge to him. He's not afraid to offer his opinion. People know who he is. He's an unexpected choice, so people will tune in to see what he has to say."

Noelle was shaking her head. "Unexpected is one way to put it. I asked Tate about him. I thought it was funny and cool that he helped you out and y'all ended up being gossip fodder, but after what Tate said, I'm not so sure anymore. He doesn't sound like the kind of guy you want to get mixed up with."

Caitlin threw up her hands. "I get that your fiancé is Mr. Sports Talk Show Host who always has an opinion, but good grief. Brady's not in the mob. He's a basketball player!"

"With a reputation for not getting along with players and team officials. Fighting. Demanding special favors. There's a reason he ended up getting traded. I don't want someone I can't count on. My show is designed to help people, not be a showcase for jerks. I'm not in the shock-for-ratings camp."

As her friend listed his faults, faults she was well aware of and had catalogued herself, Caitlin started to feel defensive. And protective.

"I know that, Noelle, and neither am I," she said with a calm she didn't feel. "You know that. But I do want this launch to go well. Syndication is as important to me as it is to you. You're not the only one with something on the line here. And I think, no I *know*, he'll be great. I can keep him in line. Besides, you're being too hard on him. I've met him, talked to him. Yes, he can be volatile." The fire in his eyes when she'd followed him after the run-in with his teammate at casino night would be forever etched in her memory. But so would the vulnerability in his voice when he asked her to be his pretend girlfriend so he could avoid a potentially explosive situation. His admittance that he was under a lot of stress. "But another word for volatile is passionate. You're the psychologist. You know that appearances can be deceiving and that people often have hidden depths. Give him a chance. A real one."

Noelle studied her. Caitlin met her gaze unflinchingly. Her best friend finally nodded. "Okay." She crossed her arms and squinted. "I'm still not happy you promised him the gig before discussing it with me though."

Caitlin grinned. Things were going to be okay. "I know, but I saw an opportunity, and I took it."

"Which is why I love you. Still…"

"Still what?" Had she read Noelle wrong? Did she have more convincing to do?

"Are you sure pretending to be his girlfriend is a good idea? I've thought about this and the potential for things to get out of hand is astronomical."

Caitlin shifted uncomfortably. "How so?"

"You could fall for him. He could hurt you. Someone could find out it was a ruse. All of the above."

"Not going to happen. Any of it. I'm not interested in him that way." She couldn't be. The potential for heartbreak was too great. "He needed something from me, and I needed something from him. Easy peasy."

Noelle's face scrunched up. "Yeah, but I'm worried."

"Don't be. I've got it covered. This is going to work. He'll be radio gold and I'll be…"

Her friend sent her an arch look. "What?"

"The best producer I know how to be and the best fake girlfriend to ever walk the earth." Caitlin held up a hand. "Within reason."

B rady walked into the studio and immediately zoomed in on Caitlin. She was standing in the back of the room, but that didn't stop him from finding her. She offered up a small wave. He made a move toward her, but another woman stepped in his path. She held out her hand. "Hi, Brady. I'm Noelle Butler. It's nice to meet you."

She was a pretty woman, no doubt, but his eyes kept straying to the woman behind her. He took Noelle's hand for a brief shake. "Pleased to meet you. I'm Brady Hudson, and I'm ready for whatever you throw at me."

She chuckled. "Follow my lead and you'll be fine. The show comes back in five minutes. I've been teasing your appearance for the past hour, so the audience is pumped to hear what you have to say. Let's get you situated. You'll need a microphone and headphones." She pointed to a chair a few feet away. "You can sit there."

As he was settling in the chair, Caitlin made her way over to him. "Hey, Brady. Thanks for coming today."

"Worried I wouldn't show up?" he asked, his lips curving in a teasing manner.

She held up her hand, her forefinger and thumb about an inch apart. "Maybe. Just a little."

"Aww, come on. I always meet my commitments."

"You seemed a little nervous when we talked about it."

Had he? He thought he'd covered it up well. How did she see what no one else did? "Pssht. I don't get nervous."

"Really?" She grabbed his hand and held it up to his face. "What's this then?"

"My hand."

"Your shaking hand."

He moved fast, standing and twisting his palm so he cradled hers and drew her in close. Her scent, the same scent that had been haunting his dreams, drifted up to him. Peaches. He loved peaches.

Dale had thrown him off his game last night with his ridiculous demand, but nowhere near as much as Caitlin had. Her mouth. His eyes lowered. If he wasn't mistaken, she was wearing the same lipstick she'd worn in the locker room. Gloss that outlined plump lips. The memory of the taste of those lips taunted him. He'd kissed his share of women. None of them had ever affected him like five-foot-two Caitlin did. Her lips parted, drawing in shallow breaths.

"Excuse me." Someone cleared her throat. Noelle.

Damn, they weren't alone. What was it about Caitlin that made him forget all about time and place? Was this pretend dating thing a good idea? He needed a clear head if he was going to accomplish his goals and get his career back on track.

But Caitlin was different. Sweet. Honest. Not interested in pumping up his ego in order to get something from him. She was genuinely interested in him and wanted him to succeed. When was the last time he could say that about a woman? Anyone, really? It didn't matter. It didn't? No, it didn't.

He stepped back and turned to the show's host. "Yes?"

Noelle's gaze drifted down to where he still held Caitlin's hand in his. Which was fine because they were pretending to date.

"Show's about to come back," Noelle said. "I'll introduce you, then I'll read a letter sent in and you can give your opinion. After that, we'll take a few calls."

Brady forced himself to let go of Caitlin. "Okay, let's do this." He took the headphones Caitlin handed him and slipped them on.

"Don't worry, you'll be great," she said with that upbeat smile of hers.

"I know."

"Ahh, there's cocky Brady." She laughed and took up her position across the table. She started fiddling with buttons on the sound board, her lips pursed in concentration, totally in her element. A few seconds later, she gave a signal to Noelle, who leaned closer to her microphone.

"Hello, everyone. I'm Noelle Butler, and if this is your first time listening, I'd like to welcome you to *Noelle Knows*. I hope you've enjoyed the first hour of the program and gotten the chance to know a little about me and the show. Hit us up on Twitter and Facebook and tell us what you think.

"As we launch this new chapter of the show's life, I thought it would be great to have a special guest to celebrate. You'll get to hear what I think every day, but it never hurts to hear the male perspective, so please welcome Brady Hudson. If that name sounds familiar, it should. Brady is the point guard for the Dallas Stampede. So, Brady, how are you doing today?"

"I'm feeling good," he said. "I'm not sure quite what I'm doing here, but I'll do my best."

Noelle laughed. "Well that's all we can ask of you. So let's get to our first letter. It comes from Maria." She held up a piece of paper. "Dear Noelle, my fiancé and I aren't on the same page about our wedding. I've been married before and want a small, intimate affair and don't want to spend a lot of money. This is his first wedding, and he grew up on the fairytales we all did and wants to throw a lavish party. Help! What do I do?"

Noelle glanced his way before answering. "Thanks for writing, Maria. I can't help but wonder if you two have different philosophies about money in general, but you didn't write about that, so we'll stick to what's in the letter. Before I give my opinion, why don't you tell us what you think, Brady?"

He shifted in his chair. Game time. He couldn't help sneaking a glance at Caitlin. She sent him a thumbs up. "Put me on the spot right off, huh?"

"The only way to do it."

"Look, Maria, you have to see this from his point of view. If he proposed, he's probably head over heels in love and wants to show you off. Most men don't propose marriage on a whim."

"So she should give in to his wishes?"

"If she loves him, yeah! Women always should." He held up a hand when Noelle's lips tightened. "Kidding. Kidding. Maria, you and your fiancé should come up with a budget separately that details how you envision the wedding. Sometimes writing things down helps you to see things more clearly. Exchange budgets and then *talk* about them. Where can you give in a little? Where can he? What are your must-haves? Are there things you can do on your own or know people who can do it?"

Noelle nodded. "I'm impressed, Mr. Hudson. Are you a wedding planner on the side?"

He chuckled. "No, just a brother who's watched two older sisters get married."

"I don't have much to add to Brady's advice," Noelle said.

"I'm a big proponent of compromise and coming up with something that will make both parties happy. There is a happy medium. You two have to commit to finding what that is. This is a good test for you before you get married. Things won't get any easier just because you say 'I do.'"

Brady settled in his chair. Okay, yeah, he could do this. Noelle had approved of his advice, and he was never short on opinions.

"Caitlin—my producer for those of you new to the show—tells me we have a lot of calls. I'm assuming they're your fans, Brady, so let's get to them. Daisy, do you have a question for Mr. Hudson?"

"Absolutely, Noelle," the caller said. "Congrats on your syndication. I've listened to the show in Dallas from the beginning, which is why I had to call in. Brady, I heard you had a new girlfriend and her name is Caitlin. Is that the same Caitlin who produces this show?"

Brady's eyes skated toward Caitlin. Her doe eyes had gone even bigger. "Daisy, you're smart and fast," he said. "Yes, I'm dating Caitlin, and yes, she is the producer of this show."

"Yes! I love being right. So tell me how you two met. I want to hear from Caitlin as well."

"I like you, Daisy," Noelle said. "You speak your mind and ask for what you want. As you know, Caitlin doesn't like to talk on the air that much, but this is a special occasion, so I think she'll be okay."

Based on the look on Caitlin's face, Brady wasn't so sure.

Caitlin struggled to keep her frustrated growl indecipherable. Daisy had bamboozled her way on to the show, claiming she wanted to ask how she could tell if the new guy she was dating was really into her. And now the other woman was demanding to hear details of her and Brady's personal life.

Brady, for his part, looked unruffled as usual. Hmmph. He was used to being the center of attention. She was not. He loved it. She did not.

But at this point, that was neither here nor there. This was live radio, and the show must go on. "Hi, Daisy," she said as pleasantly as she could. "What was the question again?"

"How did you meet Brady?"

"It's not an exciting story, I'm afraid, but my car broke down, and Brady pulled over to help."

Daisy squealed. Right into Caitlin's ear. She winced.

"How romantic," Daisy said. "So he is a gentleman. Don't hear that much about him in the media."

Caitlin glanced at Brady, who'd perked up at the compliment. "He has his moments."

"Thanks for calling, Daisy," Noelle said. "Who else do we have on the line?"

Caitlin rolled her neck. Hopefully, Daisy would be the only caller to ask about her and Brady. Except she'd been doing this too long to actually believe that. People were nosy.

"What do you like about each other?" the next caller asked, proving her right.

"Wait. I'm supposed to *like* something about my boyfriend?" she joked, ignoring the way "boyfriend" tripped off her tongue so easily. "I'm kidding, of course." She studied the man who'd starred in way too many of her dreams of late. "Brady is…" Hot. "Dedicated. Driven." His eyes were laser-focused on her, like he could see directly into her soul. Like he dared her to try to hold any secrets from him because it was impossible. He would find them all. She remembered how he'd pulled over to help a stranger. "Kind."

"So what you're saying is that he's practically perfect?"

"Yes," Brady said into the microphone, his eyes laughing.

"Um, no," Caitlin said. "He's not Mary Poppins. He has his faults. We all do."

"Like what?" Brady scoffed.

"Arrogance comes to mind," she said drily.

"You say arrogance. I say confidence," he said, playing up to their invisible audience.

Caitlin rolled her eyes. "Whatever, dude," she said.

"You had your turn. Now it's my turn," Brady said.

"Bring it. After all, I *am* practically perfect in every way."

"Really?" he asked. "Well, let's see. I like that you aren't afraid to speak your mind. You're always looking out for others."

"Thank you," Caitlin said. The compliments warmed her. They probably shouldn't have. He had to say something nice about her, but he didn't sound like he was making it up. Still, she couldn't let the compliments go to her head. She could never forget her history. Or her mom's.

"But you have faults like we all do," he continued. "You're stubborn. You don't accept help easily. Independence is great, but sometimes you can use the support. We all can."

She inclined her head. "Thanks for keeping it real."

"Always."

They shared a smile. Like they were the only two people in the room. A moment she didn't want to end.

The next listener's question jolted her out of her dreamlike state.

"So, Brady, where do you see this going? When are you going to pop the question?"

He coughed. "The question? As in, when am I going to propose marriage?"

"Yeah, that's exactly what I mean," the caller, Linda, with a thick Texan accent, said.

"Caitlin and I haven't been dating that long."

"Okay, sure, but most married men I know say that they

knew early on in their relationships with their wives that marriage was in the equation."

Caitlin held her breath. How in the world was he going to answer this?

Brady adjusted his headphones. "You're persistent. I like that. I think. You're putting me on the spot, but I've been there plenty of times before and I've always survived." He boldly met her gaze. "Caitlin is the kind of woman any man would be lucky to have. It's early days yet, but I like where things are and where they're headed."

Caitlin couldn't think, let alone speak.

"That was a fun first show, don't you think?" Caitlin asked, shutting her office door behind them.

Brady snorted. "Oh yeah, women asking about my love life. Not what I expected, but it was cool."

"No one can accuse you of not having opinions." She gestured for him to sit in one of the chairs in front of her desk.

He waited until she sat before joining her. "My mouth has gotten me in trouble more than once, but if people don't want to hear the truth, they shouldn't ask the question."

It was Caitlin's turn to nod. "I'll remember that."

He scoffed. "Like you need a reminder. You're the queen of speaking your mind."

She playfully punched his arm. "Hey, I try to be nice about it."

"It's not a complaint, trust me. When you turn pro, you think it's great to hear 'yes' all the time, but it grows old when you realize they're kissing your ass, because they're afraid of getting fired or getting kicked out of the inner circle. You don't do that and I like it, so don't stop."

A genuine smile, the one he loved to see, bloomed across

her face. "Okay, I won't."

"Did you tell Noelle what was really going on?" The talk show host had been nice, nothing he could complain about, but he'd sensed a certain reserve in her interactions with him. She was still withholding judgment.

"Of course I told her. She's my best friend."

He frowned. "Is that smart? She's trying to get a new show off the ground. No better way to do that than reveal an embarrassing piece of gossip about a famous athlete. I can see the headlines now. 'Brady Hudson pretends to have a girlfriend because he can't get a real one.'"

Caitlin shook her head. "She wouldn't do that. I trust her with my life." He remained silent. Too silent based on the way she eyed him. "Don't you have a BFF?"

"No. Stop with the sympathy shit."

"What? I didn't say anything."

"You didn't have to. I can see it on your face."

The sympathetic look didn't abate. "You have trouble trusting people, don't you?"

Yep, sure did. But how could anyone blame him? After everything he'd been through? He shrugged.

Caitlin sighed. "Fine. Be that way. But at least trust me in this. Noelle is my best friend for a reason. There's very little I could tell her that she wouldn't take to her grave if I asked her to."

"Okay. You know her better than I do."

"See. That trusting thing isn't so hard, is it?"

"Yeah, yeah." Silence fell. He glanced at his watch. "I guess I should go." He didn't want to leave her, if he was being honest with himself, but there was no reason for him to stay.

"Yeah. The show will be back in a few minutes. I need to be back before then." She led him out of her office and down the hall to the elevator. He felt eyes on them the entire way, but Caitlin's stride never faltered. "Nosy co-workers," she whispered, squeezing his hand. "Ignore them."

He could do that. In the elevator, he relaxed against the back wall, the adrenaline rush of being a guest host on live radio for the first time coming to an abrupt end. A few seconds later, they arrived at the garage level. Brady stepped out of the elevator and was immediately blinded by a light.

"Oh, my God, it really is you," someone yelped.

Click.

Brady held up a hand. "Yeah, it's me, but I might not be me in a second if you don't stop."

"Oh, sorry." The young woman, who couldn't have been older than twenty, giggled and dropped her camera to her side. Her gaze skittered to where Brady held Caitlin's hand. How had that happened?

"So, it's true," the woman said, drawing his attention back to her. "You really are dating her."

"Yes, I am," he said, stepping forward.

"Why don't you give me your number?" the other woman said with another giggle like she hadn't heard what he'd just said two seconds ago. "I'll give you mine, and we can have some fun."

Caitlin sighed. "Hello. I'm right here."

Brady shrugged when the other woman looked to him like she didn't understand why Caitlin was speaking. "She's the boss. Whatever she says, goes."

"Your loss. You're too old for me anyway." The woman flounced off.

Brady turned to Caitlin. "Staking your territory, huh?"

She glared. "Shut up, old man."

He waggled a finger. "Tsk, tsk. That's no way to treat your boyfriend, is it?"

"Keep on, and I'll show you how I'll treat you."

"Can't wait." He squeezed her hand. "But seriously don't let her bother you."

Her gaze skittered away. "Why would I? We're just playing pretend, right? There are a million more where she came from."

"Come on. I'm not like that." Except he had been once upon a time. Swapping women in and out every few months, never letting any of them get too close. Being okay with that.

"It doesn't matter."

Yes, it did. "I broke team rules by dating my last girlfriend only for her to use her connection to me to get a part-time job as a correspondent on an entertainment news show. She said it was a stepping stone to bigger and better things. I didn't fully accept that I'd been used until she cheated on me with my teammate, who, like her, was on the rise. Then I knew. I punched him and got traded."

Her eyes widening, she reached out to squeeze his hand. "Brady. I'm so sorry."

Drawn to the support in her gaze, he entwined their fingers and stepped closer. "Thanks, but it's okay."

"Good to hear."

Pounding sneakers on the pavement invaded the way-too-intimate circle they'd inadvertently drawn around themselves. Two guys, who looked to be teenagers, whipped their Stampede hats off and held them out to Brady. One of the boys thrust out a pen. "Can we have your autograph?" He sounded out of breath. "We heard you on the radio and took a chance that we would run into you if we came."

Caitlin withdrew her hand and stepped away. He curled his hand inward, missing the connection. But he shouldn't. Revealing his secrets, letting someone in, was a foreign concept to him. He didn't do vulnerable. Even if it had felt good to have Caitlin's support. He rolled his shoulders and took one of the hats and the pen. "Shouldn't you be in school? It's the middle of the day."

The boys laughed. "We're in college," the one with curly

brown hair said. "It's the beauty of setting our own schedule."

"Are you sure you're not ditching class?"

The second teenager thrust out his chest. "In this case, we can honestly say no."

Brady chuckled and scribbled his name on the brims of the hats. "Good to hear." He handed the caps back to them. The boys looked at him expectantly. "Was there something else?"

The teens looked at each other. The second, the one who'd assured Brady they hadn't skipped class, jerked his head toward Caitlin. "Can you introduce us to her? She's hot. That photo was smoking."

Brady curled an arm around her waist. "Yeah, this is Caitlin."

"Nice to meet you, gentlemen," she said with a small wave.

"Hi," the boys said in unison.

"I guess we'll go now," the curly-haired one said. "It was nice meeting you, Brady."

"It was *really* nice meeting you, Caitlin," the other teen said.

The boys high-fived each other and headed toward a beat-up sedan.

Leaving Brady alone with Caitlin. Again. A situation that was entirely too cozy and rife with possibilities. His eyes drifted to her enticing lips. Too many possibilities. He withdrew his arm. "I have to get to practice."

"Okay," she said, tucking her hair behind her ear. "Oh, and I forgot to say it earlier, but you were great today. Thanks for doing this for me."

"Strangely enough, I had fun."

Her lips curved. "It's always fun telling people what to do. Or so I've been told."

"Yeah, you're a bossy sort." He tilted his head to the side.

"Why don't you have your own show?"

She shuddered. "Oh no. That's not my thing. I like being behind the scenes, making sure everything works the way it's supposed to."

Interesting. Everything about her interested him. Something told him there was more to the story than she was letting on. But was it his place to dig it out of her? Their relationship, or acquaintance, or whatever the hell it was, wasn't supposed to be that deep. So why was he having such a hard time biting his tongue?

He didn't stop her when she headed back toward the building. When she entered the elevator, she turned and met his eyes. He didn't move as the doors slid closed. Taking her away from him. Leaving him fighting the urge to go after her.

How was he going to keep *this* from getting more complicated than it already had? Did he even want to?

Chapter Six

Caitlin collapsed against the elevator wall. What was she doing? How had she gotten involved in this—whatever this was? Keeping Brady at arm's length was getting harder and harder. And every time she was reminded why that was a good idea—hello, groupie—she was presented with ten more temptations to pursue something more with him. And resisting temptation had never been her strong suit.

She straightened when the elevator bell dinged. No matter. She didn't have time to think about her conflicted feelings anyway. *Noelle Knows* was still on the air for another hour and a half, and Noelle would be nearly ready to start her post-midpoint monologue.

Noelle sent her a questioning look when she returned to the studio, but she pretended she didn't see it and got back to work, determined not to think about Brady. Too bad listeners made that impossible by calling in and asking way too many personal questions about her love life and wondering when Brady was going to return. Which probably meant…no. Not going there.

At the end of the show, she and Noelle high-fived.

"We did it," Noelle said, wonder in her voice. "Our first syndicated show. And we had callers who weren't in Dallas *and* they said they liked the show."

Caitlin grinned. "Of course we did. We're us. Was there ever any doubt?"

The studio door opened, and Tate walked in. "Hi, ladies. Fantastic show." He held up a bottle of wine and plastic cups. "We need to celebrate today's momentous occasion."

Caitlin zeroed in on the wine bottle. The "wine" was actually sparkling juice in deference to Noelle, who didn't drink.

Noelle beamed. "Thanks, honey. Thanks for giving us the chance." In addition to hosting a sports talk show, Tate owned the station and had proposed syndication.

"I wouldn't have done it if I didn't know you would knock it out of the park, which you did."

Caitlin gave it three seconds before they were making out like the love-struck, newly engaged couple they were. She made it to two. She left them to it while she tidied the studio. When Tate and Noelle separated, he poured the juice. "I wasn't sure about Hudson, but he did great," he said, handing a cup to Caitlin.

Caitlin peered at him over the top of her cup. "I do know a thing or two about producing a show." No need for him to know that her nerves had been breakdancing from the moment Brady stepped into the studio until he offered his first bit of advice.

"That you do." Tate held up his cup. "To the both of you and *Noelle Knows*. The best is yet to come."

They clinked cups and downed the juice. Afterward, Caitlin waited outside the studio while Tate gave his fiancée just one more congratulatory kiss. If she wasn't genuinely happy for them, she'd search out the nearest garbage can to throw up in from all the lovey-doveyness. Finally, Noelle joined her and they high-fived again.

"Hey, you two."

Caitlin turned toward the woman who'd spoken and was heading their way. Deb Sanchez was a mentor to Caitlin, someone who'd been through the radio wars and come out on top. She was the station programmer of WTLK. She'd been the one to pair Noelle and Caitlin up, Noelle as a new host and Caitlin as a young, hungry producer ready to make her mark. She was enthusiastic, always scheming to make the station and its programming better. "Great show. Do you have a few minutes to talk?"

"Of course," Caitlin said. She and Noelle followed Deb into her office and settled in the chairs in front of the desk.

"I like what I heard today," Deb said. "I'm so happy for the both of you. I couldn't be prouder of what you've accomplished. Great idea to get one of, if not *the* most talked about NBA player in studio as a guest host during launch week. He was a natural."

Basking in Deb's approval, Caitlin exchanged a grin with Noelle.

"I was thinking, however."

At those seemingly innocuous words, Caitlin sat up straighter. Deb was notorious for her ideas—most of them good, none of them designed to make her employees comfortable. Successful yes, comfortable no.

"Yes?" Caitlin was pleased her voice came out strong. Sure.

"Brady giving advice was great, but no doubt the part the audience responded to the most was when he was talking about you and your relationship. When you two interacted."

"Okay," Caitlin said slowly, trying to delay the inevitable. She knew what was coming next.

"People are nosy. Y'all haven't been dating that long,

have you?"

Caitlin swallowed, panic tightening her throat. "No."

Deb clasped her hands together, the gleam in her brown eyes dangerous. To Caitlin anyway. "Perfect. Wouldn't it be great to extend his time on the show? You would still keep Love Letters to Brady as the focus of his segments, but what if you let the callers ask at least a few personal questions? Talk about what it's like to be part of a new couple and how you navigate those waters. I think people would really respond to that. Brady was obviously smitten with you. You sounded crazy about him."

Because we were acting. But, of course, Caitlin couldn't say that. So she forced the corners of her lips up.

"Doesn't that sound fabulous?"

It did. If Deb was talking about someone else. Which is why the idea had occurred to her earlier.

"What do you think, Noelle?" Deb continued. "It's your show."

Caitlin turned to Noelle. Her best friend looked nervous, but excited. Because it was a great idea. Caitlin's stomach churned.

"I'm not sure," Noelle said. Noelle wasn't into lying to her listeners. She considered her bond with them to be sacred. "I know you're not at your most comfortable being on the air."

"Well, it's just an idea. Think about it," Deb said.

"We will," Caitlin said and escaped out of the office as fast as her legs would carry her. Noelle was right behind her. They didn't speak until they'd reached the privacy of Caitlin's office.

"You don't have to do it," Noelle said.

"Why not?" Caitlin asked, crossing her arms across her chest. "I know you'd love to have Brady back. It was written all over your face when Deb brought it up."

"Because I care more about you than I do about having

him on the show again. You don't like talking on air much. Plus, I don't want to mislead my audience since you're not really dating."

"Right. We're not. Except we did have great chemistry, riffing off each other, didn't we?"

"You did," Noelle admitted.

Her pitching stomach didn't matter. She wanted the show to be successful in syndication. She wanted to prove she was a successful producer. And she and Brady were dating. Sort of. Kind of. Not really, but close enough.

Caitlin took a deep breath and said what needed to be said. "I like Deb's idea to continue to make Love Letters the focus of Brady's visits, but allow one or two personal questions to sneak in, so I shouldn't have to talk that much. People are going to continue to ask about us, no matter how much we try to steer the conversation elsewhere, and they'll just get angry if we don't talk about it for at least a little bit. Besides, it's not like Brady and I aren't spending time together, so when people ask, we can tell them about it. Keep it simple and straightforward. No need for exaggerations. I'll talk to him. He enjoyed himself today, so I'm sure he'll agree to it." She paused. "So if you're okay with it, I'm in."

Noelle nodded. "I'm in."

"Chris, what's going on with you?" Caitlin's mom, Miranda, asked, striding into her dining room. Caitlin glanced up. Her mom wore black slacks and a stylish red sweater that highlighted the sienna skin tone Caitlin and her brother had inherited from her. Always put together, that was Miranda Monroe. Even when they didn't have much, she'd made sure she and her children were never less than neat. Her mom peered over the basket of rolls she held out to her only son.

"Nothing much. Oh except for some of my students winning a contest for a video we produced in class," he so immodestly offered, taking the basket and grabbing a roll.

"Oh, honey, that's great. I'm sure the kids were excited," their mom said. She turned to head back to the kitchen, so she should have missed the smirk Christian sent Caitlin's way and Caitlin sticking her tongue out at her brother.

"I saw that," their mom said. "Behave, you two."

Caitlin met her brother's eyes, struggling not to giggle. These dinners were sacred. It had been just the three of them for as long as she could remember. Her grandparents hadn't been much interested in helping out their unwed teen daughter having babies. Though times had changed and they were all busy, they still were committed to dinner at least once a month, usually more.

Though she'd never voiced the thought out loud, she'd always felt like the lesser twin. Stupid, but true. She'd gotten great grades. Chris got stupendous grades. But she'd held her own. Until the embarrassing incident in college in which she'd openly defied her mom by dating a guy her mom disapproved of—an athlete—and the situation had blown up in her face. But that's what happened when you dated a guy who told you he was divorced, but who so wasn't. And whose wife decided she needed to sue you for breaking up her home. Ever since then, she'd felt like she was in catch-up mode to earn her mother's respect. To make her proud.

She admired her mom so much. All she'd sacrificed to make sure her children participated in the activities they wanted to, showing up to their events even when she was dead tired from working and going to school. Always willing to offer a shoulder to cry on or offering up some tough love when needed. All she'd accomplished while raising two rambunctious kids on her own. Now that she knew why her mom had reacted so strongly to her mistake in college, she felt even worse.

"Cait, I noticed you were driving your brother's Accord while he came in his Mustang," their mom said, returning with a lasagna dish. She set it on the table and took a seat next to her son and across from Caitlin.

Caitlin became engrossed in slicing a roll open and applying a pat of butter. "Yeah, my car's in the shop." She braced herself for her mother to admonish her again for throwing good money after bad when it came to Hans.

Instead her mother said, "Hmm. How are things at the station?"

Caitlin breathed a sigh of relief. "Great. Syndication is going to take the show to a whole new level. We'll reach more people and hopefully help and entertain them."

Miranda beamed. "I can't believe my baby is on a national radio show."

She took a sip of water. "More like regional, but it is really cool to get callers from all over."

"National is coming. The show is great. Other stations will be beating down your door to get you. Soon enough, Noelle's name will be up there with Dr. Laura or Dave Ramsey."

Caitlin inclined her head. "That's the hope."

"I'd like it better if it was your name under lights though," her mom said.

Caitlin carefully set her glass down, old insecurities crowding in, tightening her chest. "Mama, we've discussed this. I get as much satisfaction from being behind the microphone as Noelle does being on the air."

Miranda's lips twisted. "Hmm." They ate in silence for a few minutes. Caitlin started to relax. Then her mother spoke again. "Speaking of being in the limelight, please don't think I didn't see that photo of you kissing that basketball player." She sent a mama-knows-all look Caitlin's way.

Caitlin swallowed quickly before the piece of asparagus could get stuck in her throat. She maintained a death grip on her fork. "How did you know?"

"People couldn't wait to show the photo to me. When I say people, I mean everyone."

"Oh."

Miranda's eyebrows arched. "'Oh?' Is that all you have to say?"

"I didn't realize you'd seen it. I'm kind of at a loss for words."

"Let me help you out. Please explain to me what you were thinking. How do you even know him? Why are you on the radio practically declaring your love for him?" Her voice never rose, never changed inflection, but it never did for Miranda Monroe to get her point across. That same voice commanded attention in the boardroom as a successful attorney.

Caitlin took another sip of water while her brain worked feverishly. What to say to placate her mother? She didn't want to betray Brady's confidence. What was going on between him and Elise was no one's business. And she couldn't tell her mother about her plan to out Mack. Not yet. Not till the deed was done. She'd just have to get through this dinner. Temporary disapproval would eventually give way to praise. "I met him a few weeks ago."

"He's an *athlete*, Caitlin." "Athlete" might as well have been "cockroach" the way her mom said it.

"Yes, I know," she managed to get out of a tight throat.

"Do I need to remind you what happened the last time you went down that road?"

God, no. Her most embarrassing mistake had happened. A mistake her mother had had to extricate her from after telling Caitlin, more than once, that she didn't like her boyfriend. But Caitlin had been going through a rebellious phase, thinking she knew everything and didn't need to listen to her mom anymore. She'd been in love. What a joke. All of it. The pain had faded, but the embarrassment? That bastard continued to hang around like the last five pounds she wanted to lose.

"No, but Brady isn't like that." He wasn't. Not just words to appease her mom, but the truth, she was realizing. He'd never been anything but upfront with her. Was he always easy? No, but neither was she.

"How do you know that? You said that the last time, and look how that turned out."

Horribly. Embarrassingly. But Caitlin now knew her mom's reaction was no longer just about the stupid mistake she'd made in college. She didn't want her daughter to travel the same road she'd gone down. That didn't make her mom's disappointment any easier to take. Worse, actually.

"I'm older now and wiser. I know what to look for." What she and Brady were doing was playacting to meet larger goals for themselves.

"I know he's not good enough for my daughter."

"How can you say that? You don't even know him." Would she forever be defending him? First to Noelle and now her mom. Two of the three people who meant the most to her in the world. Who knew her best. But they didn't know Brady like she was starting to.

Her mother sniffed. "I know enough. I hope you know what you're doing. I don't think you do though."

And there was the dagger. The one that always made her feel like she would never measure up. That she would never be the daughter Miranda Monroe longed for.

Caitlin returned to her meal, the lasagna tasting like sawdust. Her mother could be disappointed. For now. The ends justified the means. When she gathered the necessary info on her father and exposed him for the fraud he was, her mom would be proud of her and forgive her for her mistakes.

It would all be worth it. She hoped.

After dinner, she and Christian left together. She looked behind her. Their mom still stood by the front door, but there was no way she could hear them. Still… "Can you meet me at my place before you go home?"

His brow furrowed. "What's up? Need me to change a lightbulb you're too short to reach?"

"Ha ha. I'm forever astounded you're not giving Kevin Hart a run for his money as a stand-up comedian."

"Only because my skills were better used elsewhere."

Caitlin rolled her eyes. "Whatever. I'll see you in a bit."

Back at her apartment, she paced. Her brother watched her from his seat on the couch, as calm as ever. "What's up?"

She took a deep breath. She couldn't hold in her secret anymore. "I found out who our father is."

"Excuse me?" Like their mother, he didn't have to raise his voice to get his point across. His entire body froze though.

"I found out who our father is," she repeated.

"How? Who is it?" Still calm, but demanding.

"Mack Jameson."

Disbelief crowded his features. "The head coach of the Stampede? You're joking, right?"

She shook her head. "I'm not." She quickly explained how she'd found the letter.

"Why haven't you said anything? Who else knows about this?"

"No one knows. I didn't say anything because I was stunned. I wanted to confront him at the Stampede event without involving you or Mama in the drama."

"But you didn't obviously."

"No. It wasn't the right time, but I found a better way.

Everyone thinks he's this great family man. I'm going to expose him for the fraud he is on zachsfacts.com. I'm going to tell everyone how he unnecessarily made us and Mama suffer because of his selfishness."

Christian rose, his movement jerky, and paced around her living room like she'd been doing a few minutes ago. This was his way. He had to think through everything before offering thoughts. Never her way, but understandable.

He stopped and stared at her with their mom's eyes. "So does your new *boyfriend* know?"

She'd expected the question. "No, he thinks I agreed to pretend to date him because I needed a radio guest. He doesn't know that I'm trying to get closer to Mack to get some more dirt on him." And she couldn't, *wouldn't* feel guilty about that. They were both getting something out of their arrangement.

"Damn it, Cait, how could you keep this from me?" Now some anger crept into the calm. "This is too much to take in all at once. I have to get out of here." He strode to the door. She didn't try to stop him. He needed alone time to process info. He always did.

She could only hope he figured it out soon and explained it to her. She followed him to the door. "This will all work out."

He stared at her silently, his anger, his frustration, his confusion all palpable. "You think so? I'm not so sure."

"It has to."

He sighed. "Look. Can you at least promise to hold off on your exposé plan until I have time to come to grips with this? This isn't just about you. This affects me, too."

Because he was right, she nodded.

Caitlin shut the door behind her brother and returned to the living room. She'd barely plopped down on the couch with a weary sigh when her phone rang. Was it her mom calling to continue the conversation from dinner? God, she hoped not.

No, that wasn't the ringtone she'd programmed for her mom. Then who was it?

She picked up the phone from the coffee table, her eyebrows raising at the name on the display. She stabbed the talk icon. "Hello."

"You called," Brady murmured in her ear.

Oh, right. She had called him earlier. She'd forgotten, thanks to the dinner from Uncomfortableland.

"Miss me already?" he continued.

"Who is this?" she asked, injecting as much pretend confusion in her voice as she could.

He chuckled, the sound sending a shiver through her. "What am I going to do with you?"

She had some ideas. Some very vivid ideas. Nope. Bad Caitlin. So bad…and hot. Warmth curled through her system. So dangerous. "I was calling to ask you a favor."

"What kind of favor?"

She rubbed her eyes and flopped back against the sofa cushion. "The listeners loved you on the show, and we're hoping you'll continue your run."

"So people can keep butting into our personal lives? Because you know that's what's going to happen."

"I know."

"And you're okay with that? I don't think so. I saw your face. And I do prefer keeping my personal life private."

"Unfortunately, it's too late for that. We already talked about our relationship on air. A photo of us kissing has spread to all corners of the world wide web."

Brady sighed. "This is getting way more complicated than I bargained for. And don't tell me pretending to date was my idea. I already know and have kicked my ass over and over for opening my big mouth."

"You kicked your own ass? You really are talented."

"And you really are a smart aleck."

"Thank you. A woman can never hear too many compliments."

"I try."

"So you'll do it then?"

He sighed again. "Only because it's you asking, and I know you wouldn't ask if it wasn't important."

"Thank you."

"Caitlin?"

"Hmm?"

"What's bothering you?"

She stared at the phone for a second. "How do you know something is bothering me?"

"I don't know. You sound tired. Not your usual energetic self."

He'd detected all that through the phone? "I had dinner with my family."

"Don't get along with them?"

She shook her head even though he couldn't see her through the phone. "No, I do for the most part."

"Then what's the problem?"

"My mother does not approve of you."

"And you live for your mother's approval." It was a statement, not a question.

"Don't say it like that. It's not a bad thing. Don't you want to make your parents proud?"

"No." So stark. Final. "I gave up on that a long time ago."

He did? Caitlin frowned. "You're happier that way?"

"Sure am," he said, his tone sure. "You only have one life to live, and you can't live it for someone else."

"Those are some profound words there, Mr. Hudson."

"Who said the only thing I knew how to do was dribble a basketball?"

His parents, maybe? She didn't ask though. She had a feeling the question wouldn't be welcomed.

"Remember what I said, okay?" he continued. "You can't live your life for someone else."

"Okay," she said. It sounded important to him that she agreed. Like he wanted her to feel better. Like he actually cared about her.

"So I have a favor to ask," he said.

She perked up. He sounded a little nervous. "What's up?"

"How do you feel about two dinners two nights in a row? Coach has invited, more like commanded, a team dinner at his house—I think in an attempt to promote team bonding or some such bullshit—"

"Brady, you know that's not bullshit."

"I don't think I've ever seen the forced bonding thing work."

"First time for everything."

"Yeah, well, in any case, all the players have to go, and we've been encouraged to bring our significant others, so will you come?"

A chance to spend more time with her father? A definite reason to get excited. Maybe she could get some dirt on him, find something in his home she could use in her story. More proof that he wasn't a candidate for Daddy of the Year.

A chance to spend more time with Brady? No need to get excited about that. But she was. Her skin buzzed with it. But surely that could be attributed to the fact that the outing would provide more fodder for the radio show. Surely.

"Count me in. We've got this."

Chapter Seven

Outside Mack's front door, Caitlin peered up at her date. His face was blank. Too blank. "Ready to do this?"

Brady tugged on his jacket sleeves. "Absolutely."

"Then stop fidgeting. And look alive. No one is going to bite." She tapped him on the chest. "I won't let them." She'd figured out—helped by some well-meaning pestering in the car on the way over—that it wasn't only Mack he was anxious about facing tonight.

"I'm not nervous. I don't do nerves. I just don't want to kill anybody tonight."

"I'm pretty sure that's why your coach set this up—to foster community. So go with it. Get to know your teammates. Think of them as people, not pieces of a possible championship puzzle. Find some common ground."

He nodded. "Right. I'm not supposed to be guarded. How am I supposed to do that if he's not interested?"

He being Lance Maguire, of course.

"I refuse to believe he's a total ass," she said. "He has to have some redeeming qualities."

"Like what?" Doubt laced his deep voice.

She searched her brain for a second, then snapped her fingers. "I saw a story on ESPN about him spending the day with a kid with cancer through the Make-a-Wish Foundation."

"Wow. Way to break out the big guns. You couldn't have said he likes Coke more than Pepsi or something?"

"No, because you would've made a smart-ass comment." He didn't deny it. "If all else fails, I have an arsenal of pirate jokes to break the ice."

"Pirate jokes?"

"Yes."

"Like what?" He crossed his arms across his chest.

"What's a pirate's favorite letter?"

His side-eye was epic. "Really? That's the best you got?"

She struggled not to laugh. "You're not answering my question."

"Because I already know the answer."

"Then tell me."

"*R*."

"No, it's *aaarrr*. Say it like a pirate."

"No." Although his lips were twitching.

"See! You think it's funny!"

"No, I think it's funny that *you* think it's funny."

She couldn't stop the giggle from escaping. Because it *was* funny. "Whatever. I have a million more where that came from."

"I can't wait to hear them."

"I'm going to pretend you're not being sarcastic."

A shout of laughter burst from Brady, his eyes crinkling at the corners, the skin stretching across his sharp cheekbones. He was so hot. She stared at him, transfixed. He was usually so contained and intense, but in this state, he was irresistible. Talking, breathing became impossible. He tapped her on the chin, the look in his eye turning serious. All of a sudden, she realized how close they were standing.

"Thanks for making me laugh," he said.

"My pleasure," she murmured, inching away from the sphere of his charisma back to the real world. Making him laugh with jokes that only five-year-olds would find funny kept her mind off her own nerves. But she would be all right. She was always all right. She took whatever life threw at her and came out on the other side. She wasn't sure what she was looking for tonight. Signs that Mack was a jerk, she guessed. A quote she could use in her story. Maybe proof that he had a ton of love children stashed all across the country. Who knew? But if she was given an opportunity to find any secrets, she would take it.

Brady rang the doorbell. A few seconds later, the door opened, and Mack stood there. The sight of him hit her squarely in the chest, making it hard to breathe, like it had the first time they'd come face to face. It wasn't obvious she was his daughter. Not to the casual observer anyway. But the shape of his nose and the curve of his jaw reminded her of her brother so much.

Mack smiled. "Hudson, right on time. I approve. And you brought your lovely girlfriend. Great to see you again. Caitlin, isn't it?"

"Yes, sir." At least her voice came out okay. No need to tip Brady off that her nerves were jangling fierce. He was sharp. Observant. "Thanks for inviting us."

"Come in. Didn't mean to leave you out on the doorstep. A few of your teammates are already here, Hudson."

They followed him into the cavernous home down the hall. Mack's wife stood at the entry into the living room. Although Caitlin had seen her in the video, she wasn't what Caitlin had imagined. She guessed she'd expected someone who physically reminded her of her mother, but Abby Jameson wasn't it. Caitlin's mom was short and petite like her. Abby was five-ten if she was a day and had a statuesque frame. "Mack, you didn't tell me others had arrived. Hi, I'm Abby."

Caitlin shook her hand. Did this woman know about the children and other woman Mack had treated so abominably? Had she chosen to look the other way because of the fame and money? Had Mack been the devoted husband to her that he claimed to be? Did it matter? No, not really. Her beef was with Mack, not his wife.

They congregated in the living room with the other players. Small talk commenced. Everyone was on their best behavior. They had to be under the sharp eye of Mack. When Tilly drew Brady aside to talk strategy about their next game, Caitlin wandered over to the fireplace. A large portrait of Mack and his family hung above the mantle. Caitlin studied the photo. She had two younger siblings she'd never met. Siblings she hadn't known existed two weeks ago. And now she stood in their shared parent's home. Could life get any crazier?

"Hi, you've been awfully quiet."

Caitlin turned to Abby, who was watching her politely. "Just a long day at work."

"But you came here tonight anyway? You're a supportive girlfriend."

Caitlin shrugged. "I try to be. He's supportive of me."

Abby smiled. "So I hear. I listened to the radio show when he was on."

Had Mack listened? "Oh. Thank you. I hope you enjoyed it."

"I did. Mack, too. Don't look surprised. Mack keeps an eye out on his players. If they're doing something that public, he knows. He encourages his players to confide in him. To trust him. That's why he insists on holding these family dinners as he calls them. That's my favorite photo," Abby said, gesturing toward the photo on the wall that had caught Caitlin's attention earlier.

"You have a beautiful family." Caitlin gave herself bonus points for sounding normal.

"Thank you."

"How long have you been married?"

"Twenty-five years."

Four years after Caitlin and her brother had been born. "Congratulations. How did you meet?"

"At a nightclub of all places. Some guy would not take no for an answer, and Mack stepped in."

"That was nice of him."

"It was. He thinks I don't know he was checking me out for most of the night prior to that, but I let the rescuer story stick."

Caitlin's lips cracked into a brief smile, the best response she could muster.

The doorbell rang, and Abby glanced around the room. "Excuse me," she said. "My husband has disappeared, it seems, so I need to get that."

"By all means. Don't worry about me."

Caitlin made her way to Brady's side. She tried not to jump when he curved his arm around her waist. Oh yeah. Pretend girlfriend. Even if he denied it, he wanted to make a good impression on his teammates. He was nervous. Concerned about how his time in Dallas was going to go. So unlike the Brady she knew from the media, but it was real. And she wanted to help him. Because she owed him, yes, for helping her out, but more importantly, because she liked him.

The arm around her waist tightened. She glanced up to him. His expression hadn't changed. Neither had his tone of voice. But something was up. She looked to the entrance of the room. Maguire and his fiancée had entered. They were speaking to one of the assistant coaches, but it was only a matter of time before he and Brady met up. Surely Maguire wouldn't try to cause any problems here under the watchful eye of his coach? Except Mack was still nowhere to be found.

Maguire and his fiancée sauntered up to them a few minutes later. Maguire smirked. "Hudson."

"Maguire," Brady answered. Polite. He could do polite even if it killed him.

"Enjoying your first Jameson Mandatory Fun Team Dinner?"

"I am."

"Surprised you're not somewhere whispering in his ear about running more plays for you."

A muscle in Brady's jaw ticked. He longed to retort. Put this asshole in his place. But where would that get him? Other than momentary satisfaction, little else. As much as it killed him, they were teammates and they needed to get along. Or at the very least, not kill each other. At least until after the season was over and they'd won a championship. Caitlin's words of advice whispered through his head. So he forced a laugh out of a throat that didn't want to cooperate. "Come on, Maguire. You know that's not my style. If I want something, I go and get it for everyone to see. Let's relax tonight. Caitlin tells me congratulations are in order. You're engaged. Why don't you introduce me to your fiancée?"

Maguire's eyes flashed, but he held out his hand. "Thanks. Patrice, Brady."

Brady shook her hand. "Nice to meet you. Lance, this is my girlfriend Caitlin."

Caitlin, for her part, looked unbothered by the undercurrents of tension. "Hi. Nice to meet you, Lance. Hi, Patrice." She gave a small wave to the other woman. "I like your dress."

"Thanks," Patrice said. "Yours is cute, too."

Stilted conversation commenced. Not even close to good, but better than open or even banked hostility. It helped to have Caitlin at his side, who had a knack for steering the conversation away from any incendiary topics and keeping things lighthearted. Soon other teammates joined them and the conversation turned to basketball, the one thing they all had in common.

"Did you see that monster dunk Kevin Durant laid out on that Kings player?" Tilly asked.

"Yeah, they've only replayed it on ESPN every three minutes since last night," Brady said. The laughter of his teammates calmed him.

"Dude, you should have seen your face when Dale ordered you to kiss Caitlin in front of everybody," Whitmore said.

"Yeah, how would you say he looked at that moment?" Tilly asked.

Whitmore stroked his chin. "Shocked?"

"Horrified?"

"Mortified." Whitmore snapped his fingers. "Yes, that's it."

"It was hilarious," Tilly said.

"It was the first time we'd seen you with something other than the Badass Brady look on your face," Whitmore said. "I thought, wow, he is human. I haven't laughed that hard in a long time."

They weren't holding Dale's display against him? No, they were giving him shit like teammates did. Brady slipped his hands into his pants pockets. "Which is why you egged him on."

"Hell, yeah," Whitmore said. "The moment was too priceless not to."

They were all laughing when Mack came out of the kitchen, his hands up. "Sorry to interrupt the good times, but I have a confession to make. Dinner was catered, but I was hoping to show off my baking skills for dessert. However, I'm afraid it's not coming out the way I'd intended."

"What are you making?" The question came from Caitlin. Brady turned to her, surprised.

"German chocolate cake," Mack said.

"That's one of my favorites." She glanced at Brady. He noted the uncertainty in her eyes before she faced Mack again. "Maybe I could take a look."

Mack held out his hand. "Oh, I couldn't impose. You're a guest."

"Don't be silly. I love to bake. And help."

"By help, she means butt in," Brady interjected.

She stuck her tongue out at him, while the others laughed.

"Well, if it's not an imposition, I'll take any assistance I can get," Mack said.

She turned to him, her eyebrows lifted in silent query. She was worried about him. About leaving him alone. He was touched, more than he could remember being in a long time. When was the last time someone had been genuinely concerned about *him* and not the basketball player who helped decide if their team won and they got to celebrate or if they kept a job coaching a team? Or, better yet, if he was going to buy them something expensive? He couldn't remember. And it felt good. Damn good.

He squeezed her waist. "Go," he said. "I've got this." And strangely enough, he meant it. She'd given him the tools to survive the night, and he would. Thanks to her.

Caitlin looked over her shoulder once more before entering the kitchen with Mack. As much as she'd tried to be there for Brady tonight, he'd been there for her tonight even if he never knew it, offering a distraction, and more importantly, a steadying presence from her nerves.

Brady smiled and gave her a little shoo motion. Right. He was okay. A grown man. Besides, her offer to help Mack wasn't about him. It was about her and her haste to get some alone time with Mack. Which meant it was time to put aside her nerves and get to it.

She shifted and found Mack watching, a small smile on his face. "You really care about him, don't you?" he asked.

She started. "Um, yes, I do."

"I can tell. Good. He's very proud, but wary. Doesn't trust easily. Holds too much in and takes too much on his shoulders. He needs someone he can relax with."

Caitlin rolled her shoulders, guilt tensing her muscles. Yes, she and Brady were in this deception together, but it extended further than Brady was aware of. And when he did find out she'd suggested the fake relationship to get near Mack? Well, she'd make him understand and do her best to keep him out of any fallout that came. Mack deserved his reputation to be besmirched. She offered up a tentative smile when she noticed Mack looking at her expectantly. "I try."

"That's all we can do," he said, his tone supportive. Almost fatherly.

Her heart clutched. How strange was life? She was alone with her father for the first time in her life. In his home. In his kitchen about to bake a cake with him. A moment that should have taken place twenty years ago. A moment she would have treasured. A moment he'd done his best to make sure never happened. She took a deep breath. But she was here now, and she would take advantage.

"Yes," she said, stepping farther into the kitchen. "Now,

how can we get dessert back on track?"

"I should have let the caterer make the dessert, but baking is my hobby, how I relax, and I thought I could handle it. But a dinner party, with a bunch of starving basketball players, probably wasn't the right time to try out a new recipe."

Caitlin was struck silent. Something she had in common with her father? Her mom had never been much of a cook, and Caitlin had assumed a lot of those duties in a bid to help her out. In the course of doing so, she'd discovered that she loved it, especially baking.

"Thanks for rescuing me. My wife offered to help, but I told her I wanted her to tend to the guests," Mack continued. He glanced at the door, then lowered his voice. "Between you and me, she's a terrific woman, but cooking is not her forte. My attempts to teach her over the years have been even more disastrous than tonight is threatening to be."

To her surprise, Caitlin found herself chuckling. Wait. What was she doing? She couldn't be bonding with this man. She was here to gather intel, not learn how devoted a husband he was. "How did you learn to cook?"

"My mother was a single woman and was often too tired to cook when she got home, so I learned how to do my best at an early age."

At the mention of his childhood, her anger came roaring back. He'd grown up in a single-parent home, knew firsthand how stressful that could be on everyone involved, and had still chosen to walk away from her and her brother? Her movements became more stilted, her smile struggling to maintain its status. "Let's get to it. What do you have?"

He paused, stared at her, considering, for a second, then shook his head. He moved to the oven and opened the door. Unfortunately, the smell that came out was not mouthwatering. Closer to tear-inducing. Caitlin coughed, while Mack sighed and shut the door. "Yeah, that's what I thought. We're up against it."

"The bad news is I don't think that's salvageable."

"But there is good news, right? Please tell me there's good news." He sent a pleading look her way.

Despite herself, Caitlin found herself chuckling again. "Yes, there's good news. I've made that cake before and, assuming you bought more ingredients than were necessary for the recipe, we should be okay."

A huge grin spread across his face. "That I did."

Caitlin walked over to the huge refrigerator. The Jamesons had spared no expense when it came to their kitchen. Stainless steel everywhere. Granite countertops. A range worthy of any five-star restaurant. "Do you mind?"

Mack spread his arms wide. "Everything in here is at your disposal. I'm only here to help. While I'm thinking about it, let me get you an apron. I don't want you to get anything on that pretty dress."

"Thanks." Caitlin rummaged in the refrigerator which was possibly as deep as she was tall and stocked with everything under the sun.

"We got used to keeping as much food around as possible with two teens who played sports and came home every night starving and woke up on weekend mornings even hungrier," Mack said.

Knowing it was expected of her, Caitlin threw a smile over her shoulder. She didn't begrudge her half-siblings their stable upbringing. But how could he talk about them, so easily and so proudly when he knew he had two others out there who'd never received that same attention from him?

Caitlin gathered the supplies she needed out of the fridge and dropped them off on the center island. She accepted a red apron from Mack and tied it around her waist, then retrieved a few more items from the refrigerator and placed them on the countertop. She studied her haul. Looked like everything was here. She'd never made a cake for forty people before, but there was nothing she liked better than a challenge. Including getting more dirt on Mack.

She'd start him off with softball questions. Get him to relax. "So where are your kids now?"

"Spread across the country in college. Eva is at Northwestern, Thomas a little closer to home at Baylor."

"So your kids are your world, huh?"

"Absolutely."

Caitlin nodded and rummaged through the cupboards for the necessary pots and pans. "Why did you decide to host these dinners? How often do you do it?"

"Each player is talented in his own way. Most are used to being the man, but that's not possible at this level. But egos are a fragile thing. You have to have team chemistry if you have any shot of winning. Talent is great and will get you far, but if everyone isn't on the same page moving in the same direction…"

"Then talent means very little," Caitlin finished.

"Exactly." Mack beamed. Her breath caught. God, that smile reminded her so much of her brother it wasn't funny.

"So when I was a player, I started having my teammates over about once a month when we weren't on the road. When I became a coach, it seemed natural to start them up again. It's a little different now that I'm the coach and in a position of authority, but I still think they're important and worthwhile. Players are more than their stats and numbers on the back of their jersey."

"Or just the guys who pass the ball or get a rebound," Caitlin added. She wished she could say she was surprised by his insight, but she wasn't. Before finding out he was her father, she'd been thrilled when the Stampede hired him last year. He was highly regarded by people in the league and the media as not only one of the best players to ever play basketball, but also one of the game's most astute coaches.

"Exactly." Mack clapped his hands. "Now tell me what to do before all those ballplayers rush in here with pitchforks."

They worked in tandem for the next few minutes, Caitlin taking the lead and Mack willingly doing her bidding. Baking soothed her, allowed her to leave all her troubles behind. This time was no different. They fell into an easy rhythm, Mack's enthusiasm matching hers.

"So what's your favorite thing to make?" he asked.

"Probably red velvet cake. It's my favorite."

"Mine, too. Even though Abby won't let me have it that often."

"Why's that?"

"Gotta watch my health. The doctors like to remind me I'm not a pro athlete anymore. So I have to monitor what I eat, Abby says."

"You love Abby a lot."

"I do."

"Did you always want to marry her? Was there someone else before her?"

"I dated yeah, but Abby was special. Made me want to be a better man. Get myself together. Made me admit that I hadn't always done the right things."

"Did you go back and fix those mistakes?"

"The best I could. Sometimes that's not possible."

It took everything in her not to stab the poor pecans she planned to use for the frosting with the knife shaking in her hand.

When they were done, the mouthwatering aroma of baking cake filled the air, rendering the acrid odor of Mack's previous attempt a distant memory.

Caitlin untied the apron and surveyed the kitchen. She'd done good. No, they'd done good. She and Mack. Her father. "The cake should be done by the time we're done with the main course."

"High five," he said, raising his hand in the air. She automatically raised her hand and slapped hands with him, laughing. "Go Stampede."

"Go Stampede," she parroted, laughing the entire way.

Her laughter cut off when she caught a glimpse of his smile. What was wrong with her? Where was her fortitude? She only had to look at the man to see her brother.

Mack deposited some dirty bowls in the dishwasher. "I know Dale can be a little pushy, but he was right. You should be in the team cookbook. I know you and Brady haven't been dating long, but I don't doubt your contribution would be the star recipe in the bunch."

Caitlin handed him a few more pans. "Thanks. I'll think about it."

The kitchen door opened, and Abby entered. "The natives are getting restless, especially because of the scents wafting out of here. Are we almost ready?"

Mack walked over to his wife. "Thanks to Caitlin, we are. We should see about adopting her or at least giving cooking lessons to the kids. Neither of them have a lick of interest in cooking," he said to her.

Oh, God, she needed to get out of there before she lost it.

Chapter Eight

"Excuse me. I need to use the bathroom." Caitlin rushed out of the kitchen, barely paying heed to Abby's call to head for the second door on the right.

She entered the room and collapsed against the door, her pulse pounding in her ears. How could one man be both caring and callous? Was any of this worth it? The highs and lows? How could she go back out there?

Caitlin sucked in a deep breath and faced herself in the mirror. *Calm down.* Just because Mack had made some careless, throwaway remarks didn't mean she had to lose her cool. Her gumption. Her control.

So she wouldn't. With a decisive nod, she exited the bathroom. And almost bumped into Brady. She jumped back and slammed a hand over her chest.

"Are you okay?" he asked, his eyebrows furrowed.

"Yeah, other than the fact you almost scared the living daylights out of me," she said.

"Mack said you looked sick."

"I'm fine. Just needed to take a trip to the restroom.

Nothing serious." She stepped around him, careful not to look him in the eye. "Let's go. I'm hungry."

They entered the dining room, where everyone else was already seated.

"Everything okay?" Mack asked from the head of the table.

"Couldn't be better," Caitlin replied, her tone as bright as she could make it. It wasn't until she was seated that she noticed she and Brady were seated directly across from Lance and Patrice. Fan-freaking-tastic.

For his part, Brady didn't look unnerved by the occurrence. For good reason, it seemed. Maguire and Patrice were on their best behavior, acting like normal, decent human beings. Maybe because Mack was only a few seats away. It didn't matter. Civility made for a much more enjoyable dinner.

"So, guys, let's talk about something that has nothing to do with basketball," Mack said.

"Yeah, let's talk about how we have a radio star in our midst," Tilly called out.

Brady shot him a narrowed-eyed glance, but Tilly just grinned and shoveled more food in his mouth.

"Yeah, you were a regular Dear Abby," Whitmore said. "Wait. Does that column still exist?"

"Doesn't matter with Hudson ready and willing to take her place," Victor said. "Tell us again how we should plan a wedding."

"You boys leave him alone. I thought he did a great job," Abby said.

"So did I," Michelle, Victor's wife, said.

"How did you get roped into appearing on the show?" Mack asked.

Brady laughed. "I wasn't roped into doing it. Caitlin was in a bind when the booked guest host backed out, so I agreed to step in. I'm never without an opinion on anything, and I enjoyed it."

His teammates looked at him with equal doses of horror, shock, and wonder. "You mean she didn't have to threaten you with bodily harm to get you to agree to it?" Victor asked.

Brady chuckled. "No. Why would you think that?"

Caitlin could see it on their faces. *Because we thought you were a selfish bastard who only cared about basketball and to hell with anyone who wasn't helping you to win games.*

"Are you sure you see something worthwhile in him, Caitlin?" Victor asked. "You weren't just making that stuff up to make him look good, were you? You can tell us if you were, you know. We're all friends here."

She eyed Brady. "Well...I hate to lie."

They broke into laughter.

"Did anyone see *Ant-Man*?" asked Patrick Griffith, another teammate. "I think it was by the same people who made *Batman*."

Brady turned to him, horror stamped on his face. "Did you really say that? *Ant-Man* is part of the Marvel world. *Batman* is DC Comics."

"You know comics?" Maguire asked, his first contribution to the conversation.

"Yeah, I've been reading them since I was a kid. My collection of first editions is my most prized possession."

"So is mine," Maguire said, looking oddly confused that they had something in common.

The rest of the evening passed uneventfully. The dessert was a huge hit. After it was consumed in its entirety, the dinner party broke up shortly thereafter.

"You are full of hidden talents," Brady said outside her apartment door. "That was the best German chocolate cake I've ever had."

His appreciation meant the world to her. "Thank you."

"Why did you offer to help? I mean, I'm glad you did, but

no one expected you to."

"Because I like to bake. And he looked so sad to be disappointing everyone."

"Well, I am forever in your debt. My teammates, too, I'm sure." He studied her. "Are you okay?"

"I'm fine," she said as convincingly as she could manage.

"You sure? You said maybe two words on the way home. Are you sure nothing happened in the kitchen? Mack didn't say or do anything rude, did he? Or Abby?"

"No," she said. Tonight when Mack said he'd righted his wrongs, that's all she needed to hear. It was a lie. He hadn't even tried. "No," she repeated when his unconvinced look remained. She reached out to squeeze his hand. A mistake. An electric current traveled up her arm. When would she learn that touching him led to nothing good? Okay, bad choice of words. Touching him definitely led to good things, but nothing safe.

Still, she didn't let go. Not even when he twisted his hand to cradle hers. "Thank you for coming with me tonight. I wouldn't have had nearly as much fun if you hadn't been there. I was able to relax. Impress my coach with my choice of girlfriend."

When had he gathered her other hand? When had he moved closer? So close that their chests were inches apart. So close she had to tilt her head back to look into his eyes that had gone dark with promise. Her eyes lowered, only to snag on his lips. Lips that she'd tasted. Lips she tasted every night in her dreams.

"You're welcome," she whispered. The only safe thing to say.

"Caitlin." He tipped her chin up.

She raised her eyes to his. The promise in his gaze teased her. Beckoned her. Dared her to take a walk on the wild side. Somehow the small space that had remained between their bodies no longer existed. She was on her toes and his head was descending. She knew before his mouth touched hers that this kiss was just for them. Real in the only way a true kiss in private could be. Not to make someone jealous, throw them off the scent, or appease them.

And it was.

The kiss was wild but not out of control. He applied just the right amount of pressure with his lips and tongue to gain the response he wanted from her. Like he wouldn't accept anything other than her total surrender to the desire binding them together. He hauled her close, making her silently curse the layers of clothes that separated them. God, how she wanted him. Now. Tonight.

He drew away slowly. If she thought about it long enough, she'd be embarrassed that it was she who clung to him, but her mind and senses were too rattled.

"What was that about?" she asked, unwilling to say good-bye to him. Needing to hear him say he was as affected by the kiss as she was.

"I wanted to know what it was like to kiss you just for us, no one else," he said, confirming her earlier thoughts.

"You were testing a theory?"

"A theory I've wondered about way too much."

"And?" she couldn't help but ask.

"Ten times better than I remembered. And you? What did you think?"

"It was…" Fantastic. Remarkable. "Good."

"Good? I can do better than that." He cupped her nape, sliding his hand into her hair and tugging her head back. She did nothing to stop him. The look in his eye told her he had one goal—to seduce.

He went to work, not in any hurry, teasing her. A slow slide of his lips against her. A small tug on her bottom lip, encouraging her to open up and let him in. She did. His tongue swept inside, causing hers to chase his. Their tongues tangled in a slow, perfectly choreographed dance. Degree by degree he took the kiss deeper, drawing her into his web of lust and desire.

Even more so when his hands joined in the action, finding their way inside her dress after finding the zipper on the side. He pushed aside her bra and cupped her breast. He murmured in approval when her nipple tightened against his palm. Squeezed harder. She gasped at the arrow of heat that landed between her legs. Her chest heaved when he drew away.

"How was that?" His voice, so deep, so enthralling, came out husky, like he too felt their insane chemistry which only got more potent each time they touched.

He'd set out to seduce. Had he succeeded? Hell, yeah. "That was…" Her eyes fluttered open. "Extraordinary."

The heat in his eyes singed her. "Invite me inside."

"That would be…" Her voice trailed off.

His lips moved across her throat. Up. Down. Sampling her like she was the rarest of delicacies. He moved to her ear and nipped the shell's sensitive flesh. He whispered against her ear. "Hot." He pressed a kiss to the base of her throat where her pulse pounded. "Fantastic."

Her moan ended on a half chuckle. "I was going to say unwise."

"I can make the most unwise decision the best decision of your life."

Of that, she had no doubt. Her body hungered for him. Urged her to give in to what they both wanted. His erection bumped against her. She wanted to touch him. Make him feel as good as he was making her feel. She cupped him through his pants. His groan was the sexiest sound she'd ever heard.

"Caitlin." His mouth found hers again. This kiss was out of control. The lust had consumed them both.

Buzz! Buzz! Her cell phone broke through her reverie. She knew that ringtone. Her mom. Caitlin jumped back, smacking her head on the door. She winced. "Ouch."

"Are you okay?" Brady asked.

She rubbed the back of her head. "Thanks for asking, but for the tenth time tonight, yes. This time I'm just embarrassed."

He stared at her, the night's shadows hiding his features. But she got the sense he saw all of her he could. All that she wanted to show him and more.

His eyes were hot, his lips parted, his hands clenched at his sides like he wanted to drag her close for another kiss. "I should go."

"Yes." Before she begged him to kiss her and do so much more. "We're just pretending, remember?" She had to, at least.

Because dating him wasn't meant to be. Even if he wasn't who everyone claimed him to be. Because what if deep down he was? She'd been down that road before and it had cost her dearly. And even if she could leave her past in the past, what about her father? She could never forget or forgive what he'd done. Getting him back for what he'd done was more important than a relationship that would surely end.

His lips rolled inward. He lowered his eyes to the ground, then raised them back to hers. One second passed, then another. Then another. "Yes, I remember. But I'm having a hard time remembering why."

He turned and walked away.

It took everything in her not to call him back. Her feelings for him were starting to feel all too real. Necessary. But they weren't. They couldn't be. Because, she, unfortunately, did remember why they were pretending.

"So any words of wisdom before I go?" Brady asked. They stood outside his car at the radio station. This was the last time she'd see him before the Stampede embarked on a three-game road trip. After taking a few Love Letters to Brady, they'd recounted their team dinner experience on the show. Neither had mentioned the scene outside her apartment because what was the point? They were friends, helping each other out. Nothing more. And she was going to continue being his friend by answering his question honestly. As a friend.

Caitlin looked up into his handsome face. "Yeah, work on the pick and roll. Sometimes, you're a tad late with the pass."

That grin that always tugged on her heart—and other body parts if she were perfectly honest—made an appearance. "Yes, Coach. Anything else?"

"Don't kill Maguire."

The grin disappeared. "We're having a mandatory Thanksgiving team dinner. What if he starts something? Isn't it my obligation to finish it?"

She smacked him on the chest. "No!"

The grin returned. "Kidding."

Her heart missed a beat. She ignored it. "Good. Now why don't you tell me what's up?"

He frowned. "What do you mean?"

"During the show and now, your ever-present cockiness was at about a five, instead of the usual 8.5."

His back went stiff. "I don't know what you're talking about."

She bit back a smile. "Let me revise my earlier estimate. Now, it's about a 9.3. What's up? Really?"

He glanced around like he was afraid someone was eavesdropping. She kept her gaze on him. Steady. Straightforward. He sighed. "The second game on the trip is in New York."

"You're nervous about facing your old team."

"I don't get nervous." Caitlin looked at him askance. "Usually," he continued. "But I am now."

"That's a perfectly legitimate feeling. There's no need to be embarrassed about it."

He shrugged. "I guess. I don't know what to expect. I gave my all to that franchise, but because of the way things ended, I don't know if the fans will cheer or boo. It's New York. It could go either way."

He stared off in the distance, his eyes cloudy with doubt. His vulnerability, the one that she'd glimpsed only sparingly, tugged at her heartstrings. This was the real Brady, who so often hid behind the I-don't-give-a-shit facade. She squeezed his hand. "You'll handle it fine either way. You're a pro. You know what you did and why you did it, so take solace in that and ball out on the court. Give them a real reason to boo you."

A smile, a genuine one, spread across his face. "Thank you for believing in me. Not everyone did or does. It means a lot to me."

He drew her into a hug. She went willingly. Road trips were a necessary evil of pro sports, but that didn't mean she wouldn't miss their conversations. Miss him. Because that's what friends did when they didn't see each other for a while.

He didn't pull away. Neither did she. Would a friend notice the hard muscles of her friend? Would she notice that he smelled incredible? How hard his chest felt? That she fit into his arms like their bodies were made for each other? That she hadn't felt this right, this good in too long to contemplate? That she didn't want the hug to end? Because it was true. All of it.

But this couldn't last, shouldn't last. So she stepped away. Forced herself to look him in the eye and smile. He didn't speak. Only studied her like he was looking for something.

What, she didn't know. "I'll see you in a few days," he said finally.

She forced her lips upward. "A few days? You're only going to be gone that long? I thought I wouldn't have to see your face for at least two weeks." She had to lighten the mood. Had to.

The corners of his eyes crinkled. "No, you're not that lucky. Thanks for the pep talk."

"That's what friends are for."

"Friends." He said the word slowly like he was testing it out, trying to decipher its meaning. "Yeah, that's what we are." He unlocked his car door. "See you in a week, *friend*."

Caitlin perused the draft of her guest column blasting Mack on her computer screen.

She was proud of what she'd written. She hadn't embellished the truth. There was no need. But she'd been as honest as she could be. She was doing the right thing. Wasn't she? Yes.

Had she left anything out? Something was missing, she felt it. She rummaged through her notes. She'd paid for a background check and used all the resources at her disposal as a radio show producer to conduct research on the man. As far as she could tell, Mack hadn't left a string of fatherless children across the country. After the dinner at his house, she'd ramped up her research. She now knew more about the man's career than he probably did. She'd combed every human interest story she'd stumbled across to see if he'd ever inadvertently mentioned her mother or her and her brother. Nada.

Her cell phone rang. She checked the screen before answering and struggled to hold back a sigh. "Hello."

"Hi, Caitlin, it's Zach Brantley. I'm calling to see how the story is coming along."

"It's coming, but it's not ready yet."

"Won't you give me a hint? Is it something about that boyfriend of yours? Do you have the real dirt on what went down in New York?"

At the mention of Brady, her heart stuttered. He wouldn't be happy with her, but he'd have to understand. She'd make him understand. "There is no real dirt."

"Too bad. He's one of the most famous, maybe infamous, players in the NBA. My site traffic would go through the roof if you wrote an exposé on him."

"That's not going to happen."

"Okay, okay. I can take a hint. But can you get what you're working on to me soon? I need to make sure it's worthy of my site. I'm getting a little impatient."

"No, really? I hadn't noticed." Caitlin didn't bother to keep the sarcasm out of her voice. "You'll get it when it's ready. Not a moment sooner. Bye."

She ended the call. The phone rang two seconds later.

Ugh. Was Zach calling again? She glared at the phone, but the scowl morphed into a broad smile when she recognized the now-familiar phone number and name on the screen.

"Hello," she answered. She hoped she didn't sound as eager as she felt.

"Good evening, Ms. Caitlin," Brady murmured, the low timbre of his voice sending a shiver through her. "How are you doing?"

Caitlin rose from her desk and headed to her sofa. "I'm good. I'd ask you the same question, but I have a feeling I know the answer."

"Why's that?"

"I don't know. Maybe because you beat the 76ers and you scored twenty-two points with nine assists last night."

"Ten assists," he said grumpily.

She laughed and settled against the sofa cushion. "I know. I was just messing with you."

"You're funny."

"I know. It's a gift. But really, to what do I owe the pleasure of this call?" Because if he said he'd been thinking about her or that he'd wanted to hear her voice, she didn't know how she'd respond.

"Because I couldn't go to bed without hearing some advice from my own personal coach."

Her shoulders deflated. Not in disappointment, of course not. No, she was simply tired of holding them up. Or something. "Oh. Well, the game was a total team effort. Your defensive rotations were crisp. The pick and roll was timed perfectly almost every time, and they couldn't do anything to stop it. So good job."

"Thanks."

Caitlin twisted her arm to read her watch. "Wait. Did you say you're about to go to bed? It's only ten p.m."

"Yeah, after I watch some film for the next game."

"You're in New York! Brady, please tell me you took advantage of an off-day and had a celebratory dinner or something with your teammates to relax."

"A few of them hit a club, but I didn't feel like it. Got to watch film. I want to be ready for the next game."

"You can't be so driven that you don't recognize that where you want to go is ultimately decided by your relationships with the players who share the court with you."

"So you want me to go out to a club and pick up a woman?"

Her reaction was instant. Her stomach tightened, her free hand balled into a fist. *Hell, no*, she wanted to shout. But she couldn't do that. Still, her answer took a few seconds to come. "No, of course not."

"Why not?" His voice demanded an answer.

She gripped the phone hard and spoke as calmly as she could manage. "Because you're supposed to be dating me."

"I'm not going out." His voice made it clear his decision was final.

Caitlin ignored the dart of happiness surging through her. "Okay. You'll be great, no matter what happens, you know."

He was silent for a few seconds. "Thanks. I'll be fine."

She wasn't sure she believed him. She wasn't sure he believed himself, but what else could she say other than "okay"?

"So what are you doing tonight? Going to a club to pick up a guy?"

She glanced at her attire. "Oh yeah. In my best sweatpants and baggy T-shirt. What man can resist me?"

"Indeed," he murmured, sounding way too sexy for her own good.

She cleared her throat. "Actually, I'm about to make the red velvet cake my mother requested for Thanksgiving."

"Hmm, sounds good. Save me some?"

"Maybe. If you beat the Knicks."

"You drive a hard bargain."

"The only way."

He chuckled. "I guess I'll let you go."

"All right."

"Good night. Oh, and, Caitlin? I called because I wanted to hear your voice." He hung up before she could answer. Good thing because she had no idea how to do so.

Chapter Nine

Brady looked around. The first time he'd ever been in the visiting locker room at Madison Square Garden. Surreal. Very surreal. He was back home. But New York wasn't home anymore. No, that honor now went to Texas. He patted the "Dallas" on the front of his jersey. The Stampede was the best team he'd been on in a long time, and he didn't want to mess this opportunity up. Despite the friction with some of his teammates, he'd never forget that the team had taken a chance on the league's bad apple.

He'd faced the media earlier, who'd been clamoring to get to him after practice. He'd obliged because what else was he supposed to do? They had a job to do, just like he did.

"How does it feel to be back going against the team that drafted you?"

"Strange, but good," he'd answered. "I had some good times here, and I'll always cherish those memories."

"How do you feel about Jesse Waters, the man who traded you?"

Brady shrugged. He longed to rip that asshole to shreds,

but that would do nothing but stir a pot that didn't need to be stirred. He had enough problems without trending on Twitter because of some off-color, though truthful, comments about the Knicks' GM. "He did what he had to do. What he thought was best for this franchise."

The reporter had nodded like she was on his side. Like they were buddies. "How do you think the fans are going to react? Do you expect booing or cheers?"

"I don't know. The one thing I can say about Knicks fans is that they are extremely passionate. I hope they understand I gave them my all the entire time I was here."

Brady rolled his shoulders in a sad attempt to loosen the tight muscles. When was the last time he'd been this nervous? He couldn't remember. He didn't do nerves. Nerves got you nowhere.

"Ready to do this?"

Brady looked up into Tilly's eyes, which were filled with way too much concern. He appreciated the sentiment, but he didn't need it. He was fine. Or he would be. He was Brady Hudson, damn it.

"I was born ready," he answered. Tilly hesitated like he expected him to say more, but he had nothing to add. His teammate finally got the message and headed to his locker to finish getting ready.

Brady took a few breaths, seeking the calm that usually settled over him before a game. Not succeeding.

"Five minutes until we head out to the court," an assistant coach called out.

Beep, beep.

Brady reached for his phone on the top shelf of the locker. And grinned when he saw he had a text from Caitlin. He opened the message with a little more eagerness than was strictly necessary.

What kind of socks does a pirate wear?

He typed back. *I have no idea.*

Arrrrgyle.

Really?

You laughed. I know you did. Kick some Knick ass tonight. They're stupid.

Brady smiled. That was his take-no-prisoners Caitlin. He texted back—*Didn't realize you had such strong feelings about them. They're not the Stampede's rivals.*

Her response came a few seconds later. *Well, how else am I supposed to feel about them when they traded one of the best players in the league? Who does that? So dumb.*

Brady laughed and typed. *So it has nothing to do with me specifically? You just think they make bad personnel decisions. Thanks?*

Whatever, dude. You're right. I don't care about you at all. What's your name again?

He laughed again. He could imagine her getting all huffy. *You can call me Boyfriend.*

Why he felt the need to point that out, he didn't know. Would she get annoyed and remind him they were pretending?

Wait. What? When did that happen?

You really want me to tell you? Because I can.

Her response came quickly. **sticks tongue out* Leave me alone. Go win your girlfriend a game.*

Now I know it's real. You're bossing me around.

Damn straight.

He laughed, the sound coming straight from his gut. He didn't even care that the teammates closest to him were looking at him like he had a screw loose. *TTYL.*

The muscles that had been so tense a few minutes ago were now loose. It was time. He stood and led his team out onto the court.

He felt it as soon as he stepped onto the arena floor.

A buzz in the building. An energy he couldn't place a

finger on. New Yorkers loved their basketball, but tonight was different. It was like they were unsure what to feel. He sure as hell didn't know what to expect.

He'd come out earlier for warmups. He'd heard some cheers, some boos. Some creative, anatomically impossible insults that only New Yorkers could come up with. But the arena had been half full. Now every seat was packed. They were going to introduce him in a minute. Every eye in the building would be on him.

Right on cue, the arena lights dimmed. He bounced on the balls of his feet, determined to turn the nerves that had begun to course through his veins into positive energy. He would be the first Stampede player introduced. "From USC, Brady Hudson," the arena announcer called out. Loud, exuberant, prolonged cheers from the sold-out crowd rained down on him.

Stunned, Brady froze. His heart stopped beating, then resumed pumping at triple its normal rate. Elation welled inside him. Blinking to hold back tears, he gazed up into the crowd and waved. To acknowledge the fans' appreciation for him. To soak it all in.

He was ready to play.

Too bad his teammates weren't. They forced passes his way even when they had open shots. He did what he could, but he was only one person. At the first timeout, with the Stampede already down eight points, he spoke—more like yelled—in the huddle. "What the hell is going on?"

"Hey, we've all been traded. We know how it is to want to show your old team what they're missing," Tilly said.

His teammates cared enough to do that? He was stunned into silence. He wiped the sweat off his face with a towel, giving himself a second to think and regain his composure. "Thanks for looking out for me, but it's not necessary." He looked each teammate in the eye. "It's about *us* getting the win, not me making a point. So let's play our game and not worry about my stats." He grinned. "Those will come on their own."

He planned to make damned sure of it. His first opportunity came right away. The Knicks double-teamed him, determined to get the ball out of his hands. But they were so busy watching him, they lost sight of Whitmore cutting to the basket. Brady whipped the ball over the heads of his opponents, including that jackass Jenkins who'd slept with his ex-girlfriend. Whitmore caught the ball in midair and slammed it home. Twenty-thousand people groaned.

Brady didn't bother hiding his grin.

The game just got better from there. With adrenaline pumping through his system, he made his next three shots and found himself slipping into the zone, where the basket looked as wide as a hula hoop and the game slowed down. He saw plays developing two steps ahead of everyone else. He had no trouble finding an open teammate to pass to at the right time or knowing the right moment to steal the ball from an unsuspecting player.

Coach took him out of the game for good early in the fourth quarter with the Stampede up by twenty.

As he exited the game, the Knicks dancers took the floor. He plopped down on the bench and grabbed a cup of Gatorade. There she was. Jessica, his ex, front and center, smiling and dancing to the song pumping through the sound system. Looked like that entertainment news show gig hadn't turned into a full-time job yet. She looked beautiful. Nothing new there. Except he didn't care. He felt nothing. Not even anger for what she'd done to him. That part of his life was over. He'd moved on. He was in a much better place.

After the game, Waters, the Knicks' GM, didn't make an appearance, but Brady didn't expect him to. Once a coward, always a coward. He met up with his old coach at midcourt, and they shook hands. He man-hugged several of his old teammates—not Jenkins, of course, because he was a cowardly jackass who'd rushed to the locker room as soon as the final buzzer sounded. But Brady didn't care. He'd said everything he'd needed to when he'd punched him. The former teammates who'd come up to him with well wishes and jokes were the ones who mattered. His stint in New York hadn't ended on a high note, but they'd had some good times, and he was pleased that they wanted to acknowledge them.

Inside the locker room, the music blared. Brady collapsed on the chair in front of his locker, exhausted. He had just enough energy to grab his phone. Absentmindedly bobbing his head to the rap song playing, he scrolled through the texts coming in faster than he could keep up, looking for one particular name. There it was. He eagerly pressed his thumb to the phone to open the message.

Told you so! Caitlin had written.

Brady laughed.

Tilly plopped down in the chair at the locker next to his. "Dude, you were laughing before the game, and you're laughing now. What's so funny?"

"My lady," Brady said proudly.

Tilly rolled his eyes. "She's got you whipped."

"Sounds like you're jealous."

"I've seen her. Hell yeah, I'm jealous."

Brady shook his head and headed to the shower, his energy restored. By the time he came back out, reporters surrounded his locker room. They eagerly parted to allow him space and then crowded in close, not caring that he was half naked.

"Did you enjoy getting revenge on the team that traded you?" a reporter from the *New York Daily News* asked.

He knew how to play the game and say a bunch of words that meant very little. "It wasn't about revenge." Much. "We needed the win. We've built up some momentum the past few games and wanted it to continue tonight."

"What about the fans?"

This he could answer 100 percent truthfully. "The fans were great. I couldn't have asked for a better reception. Knicks fans are always great. I'm happy they recognized that I played as hard as I could for them every time I stepped out on the court."

"How are you getting along with your new teammates?" another reported called out.

The question he'd been waiting for.

"Great. We've developed a great chemistry as you saw on the court tonight. If I had to be traded, I couldn't have asked to be put in a better situation than the one I'm in with the Stampede."

The reporters asked a few more questions. He said a lot of nothing until they got tired of the game and left. He finished dressing and headed out of the arena.

"What are we going to do to celebrate?" Victor asked on the team bus.

They were staying in New York tonight because they were playing the Nets tomorrow. Brady kept quiet. He wasn't sure if the invitation included him. A few teammates whispered to each other, then Whitmore turned to him. "Yo, Hudson, you lived here. Where should we go? We went out last night, but it was so boring. Last time I'm listening to Tilly. Show us the best place to party."

Unexpected pleasure rushed through him. Caitlin's assertion that he get to know his teammates outside the court played through his mind. She'd been right earlier that night, so why not? Besides, he'd had a good time at Mack's dinner party. He was feeling good after a win. He wanted to hang out and chill. The bus had pulled up to the hotel. His teammates looked at him expectantly. "Meet me in the lobby in twenty minutes, and we'll go from there."

He wasn't sure they'd show up, but he'd put it out there. Twenty minutes later, six of his teammates were in the lobby. Including Maguire. They headed to a club in Chelsea. A favorite of athletes, singers, and Hollywood actors, it was the perfect place to see and be seen. Once there, they were escorted to the VIP area. A murmur went through the crowd when they noticed who'd entered the club. They weren't alone long. A waitress wearing a skimpy skirt and a sparkly halter top sauntered up. "Can I start you guys off with a bottle of champagne? I'll be nice to you even if you beat my Knicks. You must be happy, ready to celebrate."

"We are, especially now that you're here," Whitmore said, eyeing the waitress up and down.

Brady rolled his eyes. *Save me from twenty-two-year-olds trying to run game.* He relaxed against the leather couch and observed the action. A mass of bodies writhed on the dance floor. His teammates weren't into observing. They all, with the exception of Tilly, downed the drinks the waitress brought and then abandoned him to dance and soak in the attention that came from being a pro athlete.

"Man, you were on fire tonight," Tilly said.

Brady shrugged. "Just doing what I can."

Tilly side-eyed him. "Don't try to kid a kidder. You wanted to kill them tonight."

Brady sipped his drink. "That might have entered my mind a time or two."

Tilly grinned. "That's what I thought. Now you can sit here all night, but there are women calling my name." He cupped his ear. "Can't you hear them? Tilly, Tilly, Tilly. See you later." He hopped up and headed for the crowded dance floor.

Brady nursed his drink and bobbed his head to the music. He wished Caitlin were here with him. He never failed to have fun when she was around. He definitely wouldn't mind watching her move that fantastic body of hers on the dance floor. Against him. Wherever they happened to be.

"Hey, Brady." Elise plopped down on the couch next to him.

Fuck.

How had she known they'd be there? He hadn't told her, but that didn't mean one of his teammates hadn't. Gossip was the lifeblood of a locker room. He'd avoided her so far on the road trip. He didn't know why she was traveling with the team, but it didn't matter. His luck had run out.

"Hi, Elise," he said.

"Want to dance?"

He'd been sitting here for the past thirty minutes with no inclination to dance. Nothing had changed. "No thanks. What are you doing here?"

"You mean on the trip or here in this club?"

"Both."

"I *am* the team's assistant GM. I had business to attend to here in New York with the league office. As for the club, all work and no play makes Elise a very boring girl, and we can't have that, can we?"

"I wouldn't know."

She inched closer. "Aww, Brady, no need to be so distant. I noticed that your girlfriend didn't join you on the trip. Can I hope that means that you two broke up? Please say yes."

Brady studied Elise. She was saying all the right things to entice a man, but in her eyes, he saw no emotion. No desire to be with *him*. "No," he said. "And no, I'm not going to cheat on her." He and Caitlin weren't really a couple, but being disrespectful to her wasn't an option. The extent of his adamancy surprised him, but it felt right in his gut.

She skimmed a nail down his neck in a gesture she no doubt considered seductive. He felt nothing but mild annoyance. "Sure I can't change your mind? No one has to know."

She was right. His teammates weren't watching. No one would notice if they snuck out and went back to their hotel and into the same room. It didn't matter. "You know I have a girlfriend. You're not really interested in me. You're halfheartedly going through the motions like you're playing a part. Which begs the question, why *are* you doing this?"

A stricken look flashed across her face. "Look, if you don't want to have sex, just say so. I don't need you to play shrink."

"Elise."

She leaped up from the sofa. "No, don't worry about it. I was wrong for coming." Her voice trembled. "For everything. You don't have to worry about me trying to come between you and Caitlin anymore. I'm sorry."

"Elise, wait." But she'd already disappeared through the throng on the dance floor.

Shit. He'd handled that well.

A commotion from the floor below caught his attention. "Maguire," someone shouted.

Maguire? Brady leaped from his seat and peered over the railing. Maguire was chest to chest with some guy who looked high or drunk or both. He definitely looked ready to fight as he wildly waved his hands around. He looked ridiculous standing on his toes to glare at Maguire eye to eye, but the dangerous gleam in his eye was no joke. A woman stood next to him egging him on. Fuck.

Brady raced down the stairs. He didn't know what he was going to do. Only that he needed to do something. Where the hell were the rest of his teammates? He fought his way through the crowd surrounding the combatants. They were staring each other down like two boxers at a weigh-in. Good, the situation hadn't escalated yet. Still time to get Maguire out of there before things went to hell.

"What's going on here?"

Maguire and the other guy were too busy jawing insults to answer him. The woman grabbed his arm and stared up at him with bloodshot eyes. "They're fighting over me."

Brady bit back a sigh. "Okay, time to break—"

"I'm not breaking shit up," Maguire said. "This asshole thinks he can talk to me any type of way. I'm going to prove to him he's wrong."

Brady stepped between them, the woman still clinging to his arm like a barnacle. "Let's back up and go our separate ways."

"I don't wanna," Drunk Guy slurred.

"Yeah, because you're a pussy," Maguire said.

With a loud roar, the other guy lunged for Maguire. Unfortunately, Brady still stood between them. Which left him in the perfect spot to get punched. The other guy might be drunk and off-balance, but a punch with most of his weight behind it still made an impressive impact. Brady's head snapped back. Son of a bitch. The guy came after him again, but someone—likely a bouncer based on his attire and girth—grabbed the drunk's arms from behind and pulled him away.

Camera phones were snapping away. Fucking great. Brady's face was now throbbing, but he pushed the pain aside. "We have to get out of here," he said to Maguire. Ignoring the flashes, he pried the woman's hands off him and pulled his teammate out of the club. "What the fuck were you doing?"

Petulance crowded Maguire's features. "I was just dancing when he came up to me and started yelling at me about leaving his girlfriend alone."

"And you couldn't walk away?"

"No, because I wasn't doing anything wrong. Dancing in a club isn't illegal."

Brady poked him in the chest. "What about stupid? You do know the people in there are posting photos to Twitter and Instagram as we speak, right? The money-hungry ones are calling up TMZ."

Maguire pouted like a five-year-old who'd been told he couldn't watch an extra hour of *Sesame Street* before his bedtime. "It wasn't my fault."

"Egging him on wasn't your fault?"

"He insulted my mother. He deserved it."

"Grow up! You are in a high-profile position. People are waiting for you to screw up."

"Like you?" Maguire shot back.

Brady poked him in the chest again. "Yes, exactly like me. So maybe you should listen to what I have to say."

"Whatever, man. Just because we both like comic books doesn't mean we're best friends now. Worry about yourself. I'm doing fine." Maguire stalked off down the street.

Brady considered going after him, but he wasn't his babysitter. Besides, he had his own shit to deal with. Like an eye that was pulsating like a hot poker in a fireplace. He hailed a cab and returned to the hotel. On the way, he considered calling the team trainer, but he didn't want to alert the team to what had happened before he had to. It was late, so he was able to fill his ice bucket and return to his room without encountering anyone.

He winced when the ice hit his face. "Damn it!"

This was the thanks he got for trying to hang with the fellas. Why did this shit always happen to him?

He lay on his bed for a few minutes until the ache lessened somewhat. Too bad the quiet was trying to kill him. He grabbed his phone and typed a quick message. *You up?*

The reply came a second later. *Yeah.*

He dialed before he thought better of it. "Hey."

"Hi." Caitlin sounded tired. Sleepy.

"I didn't mean to wake you up."

"It's fine. I dozed off on the couch. What's wrong?"

"What makes you think something is wrong?"

"I can hear it in your voice. The cockiness is missing."

Despite himself, he grinned. Then he winced, the motion pulling on his face.

"Brady, what's wrong?" Concern, not sleepiness, now filled her tone.

Why had he called her? The truth hit him in a flash. Because he missed her. The way she made him feel. Shit. When had he gone from wanting to concentrate solely on his career and not get involved with someone else to caring about someone and wanting her to care about him? To wanting to lean on and trust her? More importantly, what could he do to stem the tide? Did he even want to? After all, he trusted no one—and for good reason.

"Brady?"

He sighed. "I got into a fight."

"What? How? Why?" Her voice rose another octave after each question.

"I went out with my teammates—"

"Like I suggested. Oh, God. Are you okay? This is all my fault."

"It's not your fault. And I'm fine."

"Are you really fine, or are you doing that macho, pretend-I'm-fine-even-though-I'm-in-tons-of-pain thing men do?"

He chuckled, then winced at his mistake, the action pulling on his facial muscles. "I'm fine."

"I don't believe you. I want to see."

He blinked. "See? How?"

"You have an iPad or something, right?"

"Yes."

"Good. Let me get my MacBook, and we can FaceTime."

There was no point in arguing with her when she took that tone.

"Yes, Ms. Caitlin." He grabbed his tablet and opened the program. With a few taps on the screen, there she was. She looked cute. Hair mussed. No makeup. And concerned.

She gasped. "Oh, God. What happened to you?"

He told her what happened, and her features twisted in sympathy. "You were trying to help."

"Fat lot of good it did me."

"Was Maguire at least grateful?"

Brady snorted. "That word's not in his vocabulary."

"What does the other guy look like?"

"Would I look more manly if I said I beat him to a bloody pulp?"

Her eyes went wide. "No!"

"Good, because that's not what happened. He sucker punched me. The bouncer got there before I could retaliate."

Caitlin stood and began walking, holding her laptop.

"Where are you going?"

"The kitchen. I need cookies. I bake when I stress."

"You're stressed?"

She stared at the screen. "Yes! Look at your face."

"I'm all right." Her concern made him feel better. Made him glad he'd called. "What kind are you making? Say sugar."

"Why?"

"Because those are my favorite, and don't you want me to feel better?"

"You are shameless." She'd made it to the kitchen and was flipping through cabinets and yanking stuff out. "Well, I'm glad you're still alive. You have ice, right?" She took her eyes off her supplies she'd gathered for a second to peer at the computer screen.

He held the towel up.

"I wish I could do something besides make sugar cookies." She seemed to be barely paying attention to her hands as they cracked open eggs and poured them and other ingredients into a bowl.

"Distract me."

"How?"

"Take off your clothes."

She stopped stirring the bowl's contents long enough to roll her eyes at him like he'd known she would. "In your dreams, buddy."

I know, the stupid voice inside his head whispered. "Hey, you never know unless you ask."

She dropped dollops of cookie dough on the cookie sheet. "Yeah, okay. At least the game went well before the night went to hell."

"It did. Our best game this season."

"You showed the Knicks what they were missing. Suckers."

He laughed. He couldn't help himself. "You are so bloodthirsty."

"I was a Stampede fan long before you showed up." She opened the oven door and leaned over to slide the cookie sheet inside.

He stifled a groan as her shorts pulled tight over her round ass. But she only stayed in that position for a second. She rose up and faced him again. Okay, that was better. Or not. She didn't look like she was wearing a bra. Her nipples pushed against her T-shirt. Why was he noticing that? Because he was a man, and that's what men did. And she was Caitlin, and he noticed everything about her. Still, it was stupid and a complete waste of time. They weren't a thing. She'd made it clear she didn't want them to be a thing. Hell, *he* hadn't wanted them to be a thing, even though he couldn't remember why at the moment.

What color were her nipples? How would they taste?

He shifted on the bed. Now his eye wasn't the only body part throbbing.

"Earth to Brady," Caitlin said.

He shook his head. "Sorry. Just reliving the best moments

of the night. Enough about me. How's the show and syndication going?"

She leaned against the kitchen island. "Good. Our call volume is increasing every day along with our interactions on Facebook. I've been busy researching and lining up guests." A vee bisected her brow. "But I worry."

"Why?"

"Because I want this to go well. I know it's not my name on the show, but I've put a lot of blood, sweat, and tears into it, too. I believe in what Noelle does, and I want it to succeed."

"It will."

"How do you know that?"

"Because I know you, and you're nothing if not determined and focused. And dedicated."

She didn't say anything. Just sat and stared at him for a few seconds. "Thank you," she finally said. "You really are a nice guy sometimes."

For some reason, her statement stunned him. It was the second time she'd said it, and yet it still hit him like a ton of bricks. He'd been so focused for so long on his goals, vowing to let no one or anything stand in his way, that remembering to be or even wanting to be a nice guy had stopped registering on his radar. The last time he'd been a good guy, his parents had made it clear they saw him as nothing more than a human ATM. A stingy ATM, although he'd bought them a house and given them money. Nothing he'd experienced since then had made him think any differently. But she meant it. He could tell by the look in her eye. The tone of her voice. And it touched him. Way more than he was comfortable with. Even more so when it hit him that he wanted to be the man she thought he was. He let his lips curve into a playful smile. "Sometimes?"

"You have your moments. Every now and then. Once every blue moon."

She licked the remaining dough off the spoon, humming

in appreciation. Making him wish she was licking him instead. He cleared his throat. "I've been listening to the show online."

"You have? What do you think?"

"It's great." No need to mention the main reason he listened was for the off-chance he got to hear her voice.

"Thanks. The listeners *love* you. They keep asking when you're going to be back on."

He shifted on the bed. "Speaking of our deal, Elise says she's done. We don't have to pretend to date anymore."

"We don't?"

It took him a second to realize that he hadn't responded. That they were just staring at each other. "What are we doing, Caitlin?"

"I don't know, but I like it," she whispered so softly he almost didn't hear her.

"I do, too."

And that confession carried way more impact than a sucker punch.

Chapter Ten

Brady stared out the window as the Dallas skyline came into view. He'd slept to pass the time, but now he couldn't wait to get off the plane. To get back to his place and relax. To see Caitlin and not just text her or see her on a computer screen. To get a taste of her attitude. A taste of the sweetness that lay underneath.

He touched his cheek. The ice had kept the swelling down. He'd woken up that morning with a small black mark under his eye. He'd managed to avoid Mack and the team's medical personnel by being the first one on the bus and heading all the way to the back. At the arena, he'd said something about tripping over his shoes in an unfamiliar hotel room and slamming into the doorframe when the media asked. They'd left it at that. He'd repeated the story to Mack and the team trainer, all of whom accepted him at his word. Then they'd beaten the Nets and headed straight for the airport after the game.

The team was on a roll, and he had every reason to believe they would only play better as the season progressed.

He settled back in the seat and ordered himself to relax as the plane descended. Once they were on the ground, he turned on his phone. It immediately started pinging and buzzing with email, phone, and text messages. What the hell?

Brady stepped off the plane and paused. A ton of people were there to greet them. Sometimes, a fan or two greeted the airplane, but this mass of people? What the hell was going on? His eyes widened. News cameras? Yeah, a four-game winning streak was big, but nothing that demanded the media meet the plane instead of waiting until the next practice.

The journalists crowded closer when they spotted him. "Are you going to jail?" asked a reporter from a local news channel.

"Fighting over another woman, Brady?" another one called out.

"Worried about getting suspended for your latest antics?" asked another.

Fuck. How stupid could he be? He'd thought that since nothing had been said at the Nets game, that meant extracurricular activities would be kept under wraps. So stupid.

Brady kept walking. He didn't have time for the bullshit. For the digging for stories where none existed. He headed straight for his car and pretended he didn't hear his coach calling out his name. There was only so much avoiding he could do though. He'd barely stepped foot into his condo when his phone rang. He'd ignored Mack's two other calls on the short drive from the airport. "Hello."

"Get your ass to my office right now." Mack hung up the phone before Brady could answer.

Brady slammed his way out of the home he'd just entered.

Ten minutes later, Mack glowered at him from across his desk. "I don't do lies. What the hell is going on? You know what I *love* about the year we're in? No? Let me tell you. The internet. It sees all. It knows all. Until a few years ago, I was perfectly okay thinking that *T*, *M*, and *Z* were simply letters in the alphabet, but apparently, when you put them together, their superpowers activate."

Brady's jaw tightened, but he didn't say anything. Not that it was required. Mack was on a roll. "Now that they have, I'm taking calls and getting emails with some crazy footage of my star player getting in a fight in a club! It's too damn late at night for all of this. What the hell were you thinking? No, don't answer that. You weren't thinking."

The old insecurities pressed down on him. Hadn't he been here before? In the coach's office listening to a laundry list of his deficiencies. But he wouldn't show fear. He thrust his chin up. "So what? Are you going to suspend or trade me now since I didn't keep my nose clean?"

It wouldn't be the first time someone didn't have his back.

Mack stared at him incredulously. "No, I'm not going to trade you."

Thank God he was sitting down. His knees couldn't have supported him otherwise.

"I want you here," Mack continued. "You're the best damn point guard I've ever seen play, but I tell you what. I'm going to sit here until you tell me what the hell happened. I want the truth, not some cock-and-bull story you pull out of your ass."

Brady lifted his chin. "I was at the wrong place at the wrong time. That's it."

"That's it?" Mack glared.

"Yes, that's it." He refused to back down. Refused to take someone else down with him.

"So you're just going to let the media skewer you because of that lame-ass excuse?"

"I can't control what they say. I don't even want to try."

"That's your story?" Mack flung his pen down on the

desk like it disgusted him. "That's unacceptable. You need to issue a statement saying you regret your actions and that you apologize for letting the team and fans down."

"But I didn't do anything wrong."

Mack didn't respond.

Brady's stomach tightened. "But you don't believe me, do you?"

The look on his coach's face told him everything he needed to know. The memory of sitting in another office with a different disapproving team official in another city clouded his vision.

Brady jumped up. "Keep your advice. I don't need your help." He stalked out of the office, ignoring his coach's demands to come back.

"So today, Brady Hudson joins us again in studio for his weekly segment. Hello, Brady," Noelle said.

"Hi," he said to Noelle, while his attention remained focused entirely on Caitlin. He'd arrived late, and they hadn't had time to talk.

"I don't think I have to remind anyone that you've been in the news for something that occurred off the basketball court in New York a few days ago," Noelle said. "Why don't you tell us what happened in your own words?"

He turned his attention to the talk show host. "Please note this is the first and last time I plan to address this. My teammates and I went out in New York to celebrate a victory. A guy who'd had too much to drink decided he wanted to prove what a man he was, and he threw a punch. Unfortunately, I was the one he wanted to prove his manliness to."

He'd watched the video of the incident because he'd wanted to know why he was the only one taking the heat for what had transpired in the club. Whoever had sold the footage had started filming when he stepped between the drunk guy and Maguire.

"So you weren't hitting on another woman, which is what all the gossip sites are saying? That makes me feel better considering Caitlin is my best friend, and I'd have to hurt you for hurting her." She said it with a smile, but the glint in her eyes was deadly serious.

"That's a juicy story, but that's not what happened. I was in the wrong place at the wrong time."

Noelle shifted toward Caitlin. "How do you feel about this, Caitlin? What did you think when you saw that video?"

"I was shocked," she said. "You never want to see someone you care about in that position, to see him get hurt."

"Did you know what had happened? Did he call you?"

Caitlin nodded. "He did call when he got back to his hotel room that night. I felt so helpless."

"So you don't think he was cheating on you?"

"No, of course not," Caitlin said, like that was the craziest thing she'd heard all week. "He wouldn't do something like that."

"You two have certainly told a different story than the one I've read about in the media," Noelle said.

He tried not to be annoyed. He wasn't successful. "I can't control what's being reported."

After his segment ended, he and Caitlin rode the elevator down to the garage.

"What's wrong?" she asked.

"I'm fine," he said, staring straight ahead.

"Want to talk about what happened that night?"

"I'm fine." The elevator doors opened and they exited.

"You sure?"

He looked at her then, into her pretty brown eyes. Why was she pushing him on this? Despite her on-air claims, did she share her best friend's doubts about his story? His coach's doubts?

Did he want to know? No, he didn't. "Yes. I said I was done talking about this, and I am."

"You know what? I have to go back to work." She pivoted on her heel and reentered the elevator.

"Caitlin."

She didn't stop.

B rady knocked on the door. No, more like pounded. He had to get the frustration streaming through his veins out some way, and the door made for a mighty fine outlet, especially since it separated him from the person he needed to see. Now.

He'd had nothing but time to stew since his radio appearance. Before the show, he'd left practice without speaking to the reporters clamoring for a quote. Afterward, he'd returned to the gym. Usually the bounce of the ball on the wooden court and the swish of the ball through the basket soothed him. Not today.

He knocked again. His patience had run out. He would have answers, and he'd have them now.

The door wrenched open. Caitlin stood there, glaring at him. "What are you doing here, and why are you trying to beat down my door with your fist?"

He pushed his way past her into her apartment. "What the hell happened at the station?"

"I had to go back to work."

He spun to face her so fast he was surprised he didn't fall on his ass. "Really? That's the way you want to play it?"

Her facial expression remained cool. Her tone, too. "Since that's what happened, yeah, that's how I want to play it."

He didn't believe her. She'd brushed him off, just like she was doing now. "I've had the day from hell. I don't have the patience for this." He shook his head and paced for a few steps. Then he stopped, his head popping up. He sniffed the air. "What is that?"

Panic flashed in her eyes. "Wh-what are you talking about?"

But he was already exiting the living room.

"Hey, come back here."

Brady stopped at the entrance to the kitchen. Damn.

Caitlin stepped in front of him, presumably to block his view. Like that would work. He only needed to look over the top of her head. It was too late anyway. He'd seen all he needed to. His gaze dropped to the woman in front of him. Her lips had pursed in that sign of stubbornness he always viewed as way too sexy for his own good. "Got a lot going on, I see."

"It's just a cake," she muttered.

"Yeah, and two pies, and about two dozen chocolate chip cookies. Are you the room mom for a kindergartner who doesn't exist?"

She scrunched up her nose. "Ha ha. Funny."

The countertop of desserts let him know he wasn't crazy. She had been acting strange. But he still wanted answers. "You bake when you're stressed."

Her chin lifted. "I bake when I bake."

"Really? So everything's fine?"

"Yes."

"Bullshit. You don't turn into Caitlin Crocker just because. I might be a guy, but I wasn't born yesterday. Something's bothering you. I want you to tell me what it is."

"Nothing."

"Bullshit." He stared at her, then it hit him. He'd tried to reject the truth, but that was no longer an option. A sharp pain stabbed him in the chest. "Damn. You don't believe me. You think I was hitting on that woman. Do you think I called you that night so I could have a fucking alibi? That I made up everything that happened? I told you what happened."

Her eyes blazed. "No, you idiot. I'm not upset that it looked like you were fighting over another woman. I know what happened. I'm upset because you retreated. I've been there for you when you needed me as a pretend girlfriend, but more importantly as a friend." Her tone softened. "And you pushed me away after the show, and I don't know why."

His stomach cramped. He'd caused that note of hurt in her voice. "Caitlin."

She moved past him into the kitchen, and he followed her because he had no choice. He never did when it came to her. She paused at the counter. Stared down at the chocolate cake. "I took this out of the oven a few minutes ago. I'd just finished putting the frosting on when you barged in." She shook her head, then raised her gaze. "Yes, I bake when I'm stressed. I'm so mad at you, but I still let you in my apartment."

"Why?" He inched closer. He needed to be near her. To be next to her when whatever she was about to confess came out of her mouth.

"Because…because…"

"Because what?" he goaded.

Her eyes sparked fire. "Because, despite everything I've told myself, I care about you and I don't know if I should."

"You should." The words came straight from his gut.

"Why?"

"Because." He couldn't say the words, could barely believe that she meant what she'd said. But she did. It was written all over her face. He might not be comfortable with the words, but he could show her. He wrapped an arm around her waist and pulled her close.

She tasted sweet. Chocolaty, like she'd swiped a bit of the

frosting. He was hungry for her. Starving. He backed her up until she hit the counter. Good. He pressed his body against hers, her soft curves molding to him like melted butter. Yes. Exactly what he wanted, where he wanted to be. Who he wanted to be with.

He swept his tongue into her mouth, needing to be close to her in every way. Luckily for him, Caitlin was never a passive participant. Her tongue tangled with his, making demands of her own. Demands he was only too willing to meet.

All those times he'd lain awake remembering their previous kisses, denying to himself that he wanted to experience it again. His memories were shit. This was better than anything he'd imagined. Her mouth was made for his. They fit perfectly.

Caitlin. Caitlin. Her name resounded like a drum in his head. He barely held back a growl when she pulled back.

"Because what, Brady?" She stared at him, her lips parted, gasping in breath. She was really going to make him say it. But she'd been honest with him. She deserved the same consideration. And he wanted to share his deepest, most heartfelt feelings with her, something he'd never done with anyone else. He wanted that connection.

"Because I care about you, too."

Her lips split into the most beautiful smile he'd ever seen. "You do?"

"I do." Desperate for more of her, he changed the angle of the kiss, going deeper. He couldn't stop. He wanted her now. And he intended to have her. The late nights. The cold showers. The denials. They were all over. The time was now. For both of them.

Reluctantly, he tore his mouth from hers. He cupped her cheeks and tilted her face up to his. "Last chance to change your mind. Tell me to stop if you don't want this. If you don't…"

"If I don't?" she asked breathlessly, her beautiful eyes cloudy with passion.

"I'm going to make you scream."

She swallowed. "That's a pretty big boast."

"I never say anything I don't mean."

"Really? Never?" She licked her lips. Looked away for a moment like she wasn't sure what to say. He knew what she was thinking. He'd just said he cared about her and that he never lied. His pulse pounded with both anticipation and fear that she would say no thanks. Would she believe him? When she raised her face to his, he knew what decision she'd come to. She rose on her toes and whispered in his ear, "I suggest you get to it then."

Joy like he'd never felt before filled his every pore. "Yes, Ms. Caitlin."

In one motion, he stepped back, gathered her around the waist, and boosted her up to sit on the center island. He pushed aside the cake and stepped between her legs. Yes, this was better. Her lips were only a few inches away. They curled into a flirtatious grin. "You think I'm too short?"

"Yes."

"Hey!"

Again, his mouth landed on hers. Her sweet taste blurred all his senses. They were blurred further when she wrapped her legs around him and ground against his erection. "Oh, God, Brady. You make me feel—"

"I make you feel what?"

"So damned good. Like I never have before."

Another mind-blowing kiss followed. It lasted and lasted. He couldn't find it within himself to stop. Then, she slipped her hands under his T-shirt. Her soft hands on him. That's what he wanted. Almost as much as he wanted his hands on her. He gasped when she flicked one of his nipples. He broke away and grabbed the hem of her shirt and yanked it over her head. He zeroed in on her breasts covered in a red bra. The underwear needed to go. He wanted to lick the nipples that had taunted him that night in New York. He dropped his head and pressed his mouth to the smooth sienna skin above her breasts.

"Whatcha waiting for, Brady? I haven't screamed yet."

The only impetus he needed. The bra was whisked away in a nanosecond. Caitlin didn't try to cover herself. No, she leaned back on her hands, offering up the tempting mounds of her breasts, clearly not interested in playing the shy ingénue.

Worked for him.

Her nipples puckered like they were begging for his mouth. He was only too happy to oblige. Bursting with the need to do so, actually.

"Now, Brady. I can't wait." Her voice was strained. Needy. Music to his ears.

He skimmed one brown nipple with the tip of his finger, murmuring his approval and appreciation when it tightened. "Aww, baby, don't say that. That's a challenge I can't resist."

"What?" she muttered, her eyes fluttering open. "What are you doing?"

He'd already moved away. Set his sights on his prey. He reached for the cake. She rose on her elbows, her voice coming out breathless. Disbelieving. "You want to eat? Now?"

The most dangerous, sexiest smile Caitlin had ever seen in her life spread across Brady's lips. "Absolutely."

She gasped when a dollop of chocolate landed on her left nipple. Louder when his mouth covered the mound and licked. Curled around the pouting nipple. Nibbling on the chocolate, on her nipple. She grabbed the counter to stop from sliding down to the ground. He grabbed her hips and kept her anchored to the counter. His tongue swirled around and around. His tugs on her flesh sent a flash of heat straight between her legs.

Damn, he blew her mind. Every single time.

He swiped his tongue against her nipple again. Then she could no longer think. Only feel. Revel in his scent. His taste. In everything. Her eyes slid shut. Worries about what could happen no longer mattered. The time was now for them. And she would take it. Embrace it.

She didn't notice he'd divided his attention until chocolate landed on her other breast. She moaned again. He tilted her back and slowly licked the chocolate from the slope of her right breast like it was a delicacy meant to be savored. For long seconds at a time.

Her eyes fluttered open. Despite his unyielding attention, he wouldn't touch her where she longed to be touched. Her nipple strained for his attention. She'd be embarrassed by its wantonness, but how could she be? Brady was completely focused on her, the wild look in his eye enthralling her.

She wrapped her legs around his waist again and lifted her hips, grinding against his hard length, the action sending another jolt of arousal through her.

"Brady," she moaned. The cotton of her panties rubbed against his jeans. The denim abraded her inner thighs. She loved it. She wanted more. "Please."

"I know." Finally his mouth slid down. She cried out at the first touch of his talented mouth against her nipple. He gave her the attention she'd craved, licking and sucking until she didn't think she could take it anymore.

Again, she didn't realize he was multitasking until his hand landed on her inner thigh. He skimmed one finger slowly, so slowly, upward toward where she wanted to be touched the most. He skimmed the edge of her panties toward her center. He pressed the material against her. Her panties had become so damp. With want. For him. Only him. But the contact only lasted a second before he switched thighs and started his exquisite torture again. Getting close, but not close enough. She twisted, needing him. Reaching for the bliss just out of her reach.

She moaned when he broke away. Louder when his mouth landed on her throat. He nibbled, he sucked. "Brady," she whimpered. "Kiss me. Touch me."

"Are you saying that I'm not satisfying you?" he whispered against her ear.

She gulped. "I, I…" She had no clue what she was saying. Not one single, solitary clue. Thinking was beyond her at that moment. Her brain was filled solid with heat, need, and desire.

"Because I would really, really hate to disappoint you," he continued, again in that dangerous, sexy tone that sent a wave of desire rushing through her.

She gathered her faculties enough to arch an eyebrow. "Then don't."

"Them's fighting words, woman."

Her laugh was cut off when she found herself floating above the ground. What the…? He'd hoisted her off the counter. "Hey!"

He set her on her feet with a swat to her butt, then a squeeze.

"Clothes. Off." He didn't give her much time to respond. She kicked off her shoes a moment before he whipped her skirt down. Fine by her. More than.

She wanted him now. She needed him now. Was literally shaking from the need. He whipped her around so that she faced the counter.

She twisted her head around. His mouth met hers a second later. He knew how to take her higher, his tongue mating with hers expertly, drugging her senses. His sense, his taste, it all consumed her. He broke away, the desire for her crowding his face, twisting his features.

"I can taste you." His voice caressed her ear. "I love chocolate. But not as much as I love the taste of you. I can't get enough of you, baby." He nipped down her neck desperately like he couldn't get enough of any part of her.

She wanted him. It could have felt like an anonymous hookup, but it was anything but. She could feel him everywhere. He surrounded her, his front against her back. The cotton of the shirt pressing into her back, his heat seeping into her. Her hands gripped the edge of the counter. He intertwined their fingers and squeezed, connecting them even more. She ground her butt against his crotch.

She was naked. But he wasn't. His denim rubbed against the backs of her legs. He'd unzipped, pushed aside underwear. His erection pressed against her. She ground against it. She didn't care that she was the only one naked. Actually, she loved it. Felt more free, more herself than she'd felt in forever. He touched her with his fingers, zeroing in on her clit. A slight twist of his fingers left her moaning and grinding against him.

"Does that feel good?" he murmured in her ear.

"Yes."

"Are you ready for me?"

"Yes."

"Let me be the judge of that."

He sank a finger, then another, inside of her, filling her. "Does that feel good?"

She moaned even louder as he pulled his fingers out, his actions dragging against her sensitive nerve endings, releasing a fresh wave of desire in her.

"What was that?" He worked his fingers in and out, circling her clit with his other hand, then pinching it between his thumb and index finger.

Another moan was all she could manage. She gripped the counter, the tile biting into her flesh. Only his hips and hands kept her from sinking to the floor.

"Not good enough."

Suddenly the pressure was gone, leaving her bereft, teetering on the edge with no anchor. "Brady," she whimpered.

"Look at that ass. I've dreamed about it. So many times." His hand made contact, cupping her, startling her, then he smoothed the flesh. Caressed her. "Spread your legs."

She did, though it took effort, they were shaking so badly.

She heard a package rip—he'd remembered the condom, thank God—and then he was back, right where she needed him.

He gripped her hips, his fingers biting into her flesh, and tilted them upward. He sank into her in one long thrust that left her quaking.

"Do you lie awake at night thinking how good it would feel to have me inside you like I do?" he whispered in her ear, sliding out and sliding back in a powerful thrust, awakening all of her nerve endings. He gripped her hips harder when she didn't answer. He stopped moving, leaving her dangling on the cusp of something extraordinary. "Do you?"

"Yes," she released on a shaky breath.

"How does the reality feel?"

"Good." All she would offer. Challenging him. Wanting him to admit to feeling as out of control as she did.

"That's it? I can do better." He slid his hands up her body and cupped her breasts. Rolling her nipples between them. Tugging on them, sending a spike of arousal through her body. A little harder when she pushed her chest into his hands, the pinch of pain ratcheting up her desire. She couldn't get enough of his actions. She was a mass of desire.

He chuckled and tugged again. He thrust inside her. "I can feel you surrounding me. Hugging me. It feels so damn good I can barely stand it. Can you feel me deep inside you?"

"Yes." He filled her. Made her feel complete. Whole. She

licked her lips. "Brady?"

"Hmm?" He flexed his hips.

A burst of pleasure almost waylaid her. "I-I…can't wait anymore."

"Yes, you can. I don't want this to end. I've dreamed of it too long."

He slowly slid out of her, scraping against her sensitive flesh, then back inside. Over and over again in an unrelenting pattern. Driving her out of her mind. But no more than she was doing to him. His voice was strained. His breaths came hard and fast. She concentrated on his hand tracking down her quivering stomach. The skin of his hand pulled tight over the bone like he was at the edge of his control. They were in this together. His hand delved, homing in on her clit. Driving them closer to the edge.

"Brady!"

"Come for me, Caitlin." His command was accompanied by a twist of his hips. She screamed as the tidal wave swept over her. His hoarse shout in her ear a second later was all she'd longed to hear and more.

Chapter Eleven

"So, umm, yeah." That sex afterglow didn't last long enough, especially when you were standing in your kitchen naked while your partner only needed to adjust a few things to be fully clothed. Or when said partner didn't take his dark, glittering gaze off you while he did said adjusting. A gaze that reminded you how he made you feel. Sexy. Wanted. So maybe there was a little bit of glow left.

She turned in a circle searching for her panties, but her eyesight wasn't at its best at the moment. Not to mention that her limbs were still shaking and she no longer had Brady's support to keep her from sliding to the floor. And her mind still whirred from what had just happened. The best sex of her life. With the guy she wasn't supposed to be getting involved with. Who'd given her an orgasm she would never ever forget.

Memories consumed her. Fine. The glow thrived.

What was she doing again? Oh, yeah. Looking for her clothes. She still couldn't find her underwear, so she settled for grabbing her skirt and stepping into it. She snatched the shirt Brady held out to her and yanked it over her head. "Thanks.

Um, want some sugar cookies? I saved you some."

"They can wait."

"Oh, okay."

"Want to tell me why you're back to not looking at me?"

She spun. "I am looking at you."

His eyebrows lifted. Waiting. Not giving an inch.

"It's just…"

"What?"

She shrugged. "We had sex, which was…"

"Amazing?"

A brief smile tugged at her lips. "Yeah, but that wasn't my point."

"Then what was?"

"I told you I cared about you, and you said you cared about me."

His eyebrows drew together. "I do care about you. I think about you when we're apart. I missed you when I was on the road trip. I live for your texts. For your calls. For your insults and backhanded compliments."

She smiled. How could she not? He always made her smile. Always made her happy. "I try my best." Her smile faded. "Why did you push me away at the station? I still can't forget that."

He took a deep breath, shadows creeping into his dark chocolate eyes. "When we got back from the trip, Mack called me into his office. It didn't end well. He wanted to know the whole story, and I didn't tell him. I saw that same doubt in Noelle's face that I saw in his. When you kept asking me about New York, I thought it meant you didn't trust me either, and I shut down."

"No, I kept asking because you looked so lost." God, she hated defending Mack, but he'd left her with no choice. "Are you sure that wasn't your coach's motivation, as well? To get the truth, so he could help you."

Brady blinked like the thought had never occurred to him. "I…don't know."

She reached out for his hand. "Why haven't you defended yourself in public? Told the whole story? Noelle was right in one regard. Everyone thinks you're a troublemaker because of the media reports."

Brady sighed and rubbed the back of his neck. "It was my fault we went to the club."

"You couldn't have known some drunk guy was going to be there looking for a fight."

"Yeah, but I should have kept a better look out for my teammates."

"They're grown men."

"I know, but I feel like I've found something here with the Stampede. Something worth fighting for. I'll be okay. Another scandal will occur in the next few days, and the media will forget about me. And this way, Maguire won't get in trouble with his fiancée."

She threw her hands up in the air. "Gah. There you go being nice again. I can't resist you when you act like that."

"Good. Exactly what I wanted to hear. Where do we go from here?"

Her eyes widened. "What do you mean?"

He looked resolute. "I distinctly remember us both saying we cared about the other more than once."

"You mean the orgasm didn't obliterate all your brain cells?"

The corner of his mouth lifted. "Most of them, but I have a few left." His face went serious again. "You know you could act a little happier about this turn of events."

She reached for his hand and gestured for him to sit at the kitchen table. "It's not you. It's me."

"If you're going to tell me you didn't mean it and break up with me, couldn't you at least come up with something a little more original?" He said it in a joking manner, but he couldn't hide the hint of vulnerability that crept into his voice.

She settled on his lap and caressed his strong jaw. "I'm not breaking up with you."

"Then what's the deal? And don't deny that there is a deal. It's written all over your face."

Caitlin drew in a deep breath. She wanted this man in her life. As much as it pained her to dredge up the past, he deserved to know why she was so reticent. At least part of the reason. "When I was in college, I met a guy. A pro football player."

Brady shifted. "Okay."

"It was great. He was great. My mom was against the relationship, said she didn't trust him, but I was twenty years old and thought I knew everything. She couldn't give any solid reason why she didn't like him, and I clung to him even harder, which he loved and encouraged."

"What happened?"

She dropped her head against his shoulder. Being with him, knowing he had her back, comforted her. Made telling the story a little easier. "More like what didn't happen. I'll never forget getting a phone call from his wife calling me all kinds of names."

"What?"

"Oh, yeah. He played in Dallas, but left his young family in Florida because he didn't want to uproot them. Or at least that's what he told his wife. I was such an idiot. I never questioned anything he told me. Never googled him. When I met him, he told me he was divorced. But there was no divorce. Not until I came into the picture anyway." Caitlin closed her eyes for a second. Forced out the rest of the embarrassing tale. "His wife tried to sue me for breaking up her home. That was the icing on the cake of humiliation."

His hold on her tightened. "What happened?"

"My mom is a lawyer, and she called in some favors at her firm. It all went away, but until it did, it was awful. He was a second-string player, so the story didn't gain much traction nationally, but people here would say horrible things. It's why I don't like being the center of attention."

"Who was it? I'll kick his ass." The threat in his voice was real.

She shook her head. "It doesn't matter. He's long gone and not on the team anymore."

"It does matter if he's the reason you're keeping me at arm's length."

"I'm not."

"You sure?"

Caitlin looked down at her hands. She didn't know how to answer that.

"I'm not him," he said quietly.

Her head jerked up. "I know, but…"

"But what?"

"What if you break my heart?" She spoke so softly she wasn't sure he heard her.

"What if you break mine?"

"What? I'd never do that." The thought had never occurred to her. That she could hurt him.

"Then don't shut me out. You said you didn't like it when I did it earlier, and I don't like when you do it. Yes, I have a past. But that's what it is. A past. I've grown up. I want to be with you and only you. I'm in. All the way. Are you?"

She searched his eyes. Sincerity shone there. She gave him the only answer she could. "Yes. I want to be with you. Let's see where this goes."

A dazzling smile broke across his face. "I'm glad I found someone I can really talk to and trust."

She bit her lip, uneasiness gathering inside. She had to tell him about her connection to Mack. "About that."

"Nope." He nibbled at her neck. "You agreed to give us a try. No more doom tonight." He pressed a hot kiss to the spot where her neck met her shoulder.

"Ahh…"

He swept her up in his arms, his eyes dark and sexy. "Where's the bedroom, Ms. Caitlin?"

Later. She would tell him later.

Caitlin stared at the brightly wrapped package in Brady's hand, afraid to touch it like it would reach out and bite her. "What's that?"

He leaned in for a kiss. A small brush of lips, but more than enough to turn her insides out. As usual. "Hello to you, too. Are you going to let me in?"

Her eyes fluttered open to meet his amused gaze. She stepped back. "Oh, yeah. Sorry. Come in." She kept a wary eye on the package as she followed him into her apartment.

"I bought you this." He held out the present. "I saw it in Target and couldn't resist."

She paused. "You go to Target?"

"Doesn't everybody? Now stop stalling and open it."

She took the offering with shaking hands, unwrapped it, and laughed. This is why she'd been afraid. Because he was starting to know her too well.

"I know you're always worried about ratings, so what better way to get people listening?"

She sent a look his way. "With *Yo-Ho-Ha-Ha-Ha!: A Pirate Joke Book*?"

"Yeah, they'll laugh and tell their friends."

Her heart took a swan dive to land at his feet. "Why did you buy this?"

"To see that smile on your face."

No doubt the joy blooming in her heart had manifested itself on her face. How could it not? She froze. Wait. What was he doing? "Are you *wooing* me?"

"Yes."

She blinked. The way he said it. Like it was obvious. Like he had no hesitation about what he was doing. It concerned her. Okay, scared the crap out of her. She was supposed to be seeing where this thing between them went. Slowly. He wasn't interested in slow. No, not the man who played basketball at one hundred miles per hour. She couldn't keep up.

Trust came slowly for her. She didn't jump headfirst into relationships with men who weren't suitable. Even though they'd both admitted to having feelings for each other, it was hard to throw away years of conditioning. Panic seized her heart. Sweat broke out on her palms. "Stop."

"Why? I know you like it."

"I do not." Except she did. Way, way too much. She took a deep breath. "I'm being rude. Thank you for the book. I"— *love*—"really like it." It was so her. She stared at the book with Spongebob Squarepants in a bandanna and eye patch taking center stage on the cover.

Oh God, they'd gotten to the stage where they had inside jokes. When? How?

"I'm glad. Although I wouldn't be upset if you cracked a smile. Or sounded a little more excited."

"Showed my appreciation?" She closed the gap between them and rose on her toes. Kissing him never got old. How could it when he was a genius at it? Slow and steady. Teasing her with a small nip to her bottom lip which led to her chasing him. Led to her moaning when their tongues met. She only came up for air when her phone rang. "Hold that thought."

She reluctantly stepped away and grabbed her phone. And scrunched her nose when she saw who was calling. With a sigh, she answered. "Hello."

She conversed for a few minutes, only offering a few "I sees" and "okays" at the appropriate intervals. She moved a few feet away to her desk in the living room and picked up a sheet of paper, frowned, and nodded some more. She ended the call a minute later.

Brady was watching with concern on his face. "Everything okay?"

She rubbed her eyes. "Um, yeah. I guess."

An eyebrow lifted. "It's not possible to sound less convincing. Want to try again?"

"It's not anything serious. Ugh. The mechanic is getting a little annoyed that I haven't committed to all the repairs. I keep dragging my feet on all the stuff the car needs done to it. But I can't keep borrowing my brother's car forever, I guess."

He frowned. "Do you not have the money to get it fixed? Do you need a loan?"

She recoiled in horror. "What? No!"

"To which part?"

"All of it. I don't want or need your money."

"Then why don't you get your car fixed? Or better yet get a new one? From what I remember, Hans was on his last legs. It's not shameful to admit you need some help."

Caitlin spoke through gritted teeth. "For the last time, I don't need your help. I'm fine."

"Then what's the problem?"

Why wouldn't he let this go? Based on the mutinous expression on his face, he had no plans of doing so anytime soon. Caitlin sighed. "I grew up without a lot of money. My mom was great, but money was tight."

"Okay. I get that. I grew up the same way."

"Right. Because of it, I have a hard time letting go of money because you never know when you'll need it. So I keep as much of my money as I can. I bought Hans only after finding a ridiculously good deal on it."

He studied her. "I get that. So you have some money saved?"

"Yes."

"Enough for a down payment for a new car?"

"Yes," she said, her voice going small.

"More than that?"

Caitlin hesitated. "Yes."

"How much more?"

"I have a car fund."

"Outside your retirement and other savings?"

Her chin lifted. "Yes."

"How much is in the fund?"

She swallowed. His gaze refused to let her back away and not answer. "Enough to buy a new car," she whispered.

He nodded slowly as though expecting the answer. "And you don't want to use it even though I have no doubt you are fully on track for retirement, correct?"

"Yes." His calmness only served to agitate her. "What if I need it? You never know what the future holds. What if the ratings for the show go in the toilet in the new cities? What if I get fired tomorrow?"

He side-eyed her. "The best producer in the game is not going to get fired tomorrow."

His confident tone coaxed a smile out of her. "The best producer? You know a lot of producers?"

"Just one, but she was smart enough to hire me for a segment on her show, so that obviously makes her the brightest and the best." He smiled, highlighting his sharp cheekbones, but the serious look on his face told her he believed in her.

Caitlin laughed. He had a way of making her do that on a regular basis.

He clapped his hands. "Change of plans. Instead of dinner and a movie, I'll take you car shopping."

Her laughter cut off. "Wait. What? You'll do no such thing. I'll get my car fixed, and I'll be fine."

"Caitlin, you're throwing good money after bad." He pointed to the paper she still held. "Look at that estimate. Those are just the most serious repairs. I'm sure there's a whole list of other recommended repairs, too."

She hid the invoice behind her back. His look told her it was too late.

"I know you're concerned about spending money," he said. "But I'm concerned about you being stranded on the side of the road somewhere, and it not being me who pulls over to help you. You have the same concerns, too. Don't think I've forgotten how you basically accused me of being a serial killer."

Damn it, she hated when he was right. But she kept her mouth shut. It was one thing to think he was right, it was another to open her mouth and let him know it.

"Not going to say anything, huh?" he asked. He cupped her shoulders with his big hands and squeezed. "Look, I understand being poor and the fear that comes with not being sure where your next meal is coming from or if your parents have enough gas in the car to get you to school and them to work. That's part of the reason I was so obsessed with basketball. But you can't let fear win and overrule good sense. You know that. That's why you have a new car fund in the first place." He grabbed her purse off the coffee table. "Let's go."

"Hey, give that back!"

"Not until we pull into a car dealership and you actually look at a car."

He held the bag above his head. She glared at him. She would not jump like a dog. She had too much respect for herself. Besides, even if she did, she wouldn't be able to grab the purse. Being short sucked monkey balls sometimes. Instead, she lifted her chin. "Fine. Let's go."

She marched to the door and ignored his low chuckle behind her. She didn't speak to him when they arrived at his

Porsche or when he unlocked the door and she got in.

"What kind of car do you want?" he asked after he slid in.

"Probably a Toyota," she mumbled.

"Been doing some research?" he asked, the laughter silent but heard all the same.

"Yes. Leave me alone."

"I wouldn't dream of messing with you."

"Unless it's bullying me into going car shopping."

"It's for your own good."

"Leave me alone."

"Yes, Ms. Caitlin." Amusement colored his tone.

She knew she was being silly. This was precisely the reason she'd been saving for a car. And doing research on the car that would offer the best combination of good gas mileage, safety features, and reliability. But letting go of her money, knowing she'd never have it again, made her anxious.

They didn't speak again until he pulled into the dealership a few blocks from her place. He shifted toward her. "Ready?"

"Sure." Maybe.

She stepped out of the car. Shiny cars in a variety of hues filled the lot as far as the eye could see. A fire-engine red sedan caught her eye. It sparkled underneath the bright sun like it had known she was coming, and it was making its best effort to impress her. She found herself in front of it, her hands balled into fists at her sides. It was so pretty and shiny, she almost didn't want to touch it. Thanks to her research, she already knew all its specs and what it could do. The only thing she didn't know was how she would feel behind the wheel. Great, she didn't doubt, but she wanted to test her theory out to make sure.

Brady didn't say anything as she prowled around the pretty, pretty car, studying it from every angle. She maintained her dignity by not pressing her face to the glass to look inside. Dignity, she had it. In tiny, tiny amounts. But the car was so pretty.

An hour later, she drove off in a brand-new car.

And she had Brady to thank for pushing her to do what needed to be done. If it weren't for him, she'd still be trying to get Hans to work while her money didn't do what she'd intended for it to do. He'd acknowledged her concerns without belittling them, but still giving her the tough love everyone could use every now and then.

What was she going to do about him? About them? About the fact that her plans to take things slowly had no chance in hell of withstanding the Brady onslaught? Not with the feelings he awakened in her. And if she looked closely into his eyes, the feelings she'd awakened in him.

But she could obsess about that later. She cranked up the radio in her brand-new car. When she arrived back at her apartment complex, she parked next to Brady. He'd already gotten out of his Porsche. She jumped out of her car. "Thank you for making me go and stare down my fears." She ran around to caress the bumper. "I'm so excited! Look at my baby."

"Why am I jealous of a car?" he grumbled.

"Aww, you don't have to be jealous. I wouldn't have her without you."

"Yeah?" He snagged her belt loop with a finger and drew her closer.

"Yeah," she murmured against his neck, wanting a taste. Just a small one. He smelled so good. She inhaled the spicy scent she would forever associate with him.

"Why don't you bring your mouth to the left?" he whispered.

She did just that. His mouth, that talented eighth wonder of the world, was waiting. She got lost in him, in how he made her feel.

"Let's take this inside," he said.

"Good idea."

"Caitlin." Her mother appeared out of nowhere. Okay, that wasn't exactly true. She'd gotten so wrapped up in Brady, she hadn't heard her mom approach. Her mom's eyes immediately homed in on the spot where Brady's hand rested possessively at Caitlin's hip.

Caitlin froze. Fought the impulse to move away from the man at her side. "Mama, what are you doing here?"

Her mother adjusted the designer handbag on her shoulder. She was impeccably dressed as always in trouser jeans and a sleek green sweater, a matching scarf shot with gold loosely tied around her neck. "I didn't realize I couldn't visit my only daughter."

Guilt wormed its way into Caitlin's heart. "Of course you can. You usually call first, that's all."

"I thought I'd surprise you. I was on my way to the mall and thought I'd see if you'd like to join me. Looks like I'm the one to get a surprise."

"Brady and I went car shopping," Caitlin said inanely.

"You did?" Surprise flashed across her mom's face. She peered behind them. "I see you did. I assume the Toyota is yours and not the Porsche."

"Right."

Her mother returned her attention to her daughter.

"I'm sorry. Where are my manners?" Probably buried underneath the chaos running rampant through her brain. "Mama, this is Brady Hudson. Brady, this is my mother, Miranda Monroe."

"It's nice to meet you, Ms. Monroe." Brady held out his hand.

To Caitlin's relief, her mom didn't hesitate in taking it. "Likewise. I thought I recognized you from that photo in which you seemed to be *very* interested in my daughter in a very public place."

"Mama." *Concrete, please open up and swallow me whole.*

To his credit, Brady didn't flinch. "Yes, that photo was unfortunate. I didn't realize someone was out there."

"Maybe you should have," her mother returned coolly. "You are a public figure. People are always watching."

"Indeed." Brownie points to Brady for not rising to the bait. He clapped his hands together. "It's getting late. Why don't I take you two to dinner, if you don't mind me horning in on mother-daughter time?"

"That would be excellent." To Caitlin's utter shock and amazement, that statement came from her mom.

They agreed on an Italian restaurant a few blocks away from Caitlin's apartment. Unfortunately, that was the last smooth interaction. They'd barely sat at their table at the restaurant when Miranda spoke.

"Are you toying with my daughter, Mr. Hudson?" It didn't seem to occur to her mother that Brady was a foot taller and over one hundred pounds heavier than she was. "How many other women are you seeing or should I say sleeping with? You did get into a fight over a woman who isn't my daughter at a nightclub recently, didn't you?"

"Mama!" Caitlin stared at her in horror.

Brady squeezed her leg under the table. "It's okay. No, I didn't get into a fight at a club over another woman. That was a misunderstanding. No, I'm not seeing anyone else and no, I'm not toying with your daughter."

"Talk is cheap," her mom said, her tone casual like they were discussing the weather.

"Indeed it is. Only time and my actions will tell."

"You are correct." Her mother picked up her menu and serenely inspected it like she hadn't engaged in a verbal smackdown.

The rest of the dinner passed uneventfully. Miranda was unfailingly polite, but inaccessible, offering only tepid responses.

"I'm sorry about my mom," Caitlin said later that night back at her apartment.

Brady shrugged. "She's reserving judgment."

Caitlin snorted. "Is that what we're calling it?"

He lifted her chin with one hand while drawing her close with the other arm around her waist. "Here's the deal. Ultimately, it doesn't matter what she thinks. It matters what you think."

"She's my mother." *Please understand*, she pleaded with him silently. A message he didn't seem interested in receiving.

He frowned. "And? She can't control you forever. You're an adult. You have no problem telling me what's on your mind. Why aren't you like that with her?"

"I don't want to let her down again. I got involved with an athlete, and it blew up in my face. She was always there for me. Still is."

"So you're going to break up with me if she tells you to?"

"No. It's just—that time was so crazy. I felt like the biggest fool."

"Don't you think it's time to forgive yourself?"

She shook her head. "I almost ruined a marriage. My mom tried to warn me about him, but I didn't listen."

"One of the things I admire about you is that you put others first, but that doesn't mean you should let your mom rule your life."

"Brady."

"Look, I get wanting your parent's approval. I was never what my parents wanted. Look, I get wanting your mom's approval, but I also know you have to give up on that dream at some point. I was always drawn to basketball. It made me happy and I was good at it. My parents tolerated basketball, but no more than that. They resented the money it cost, the time it took. I got it. We didn't have a lot of money, but I thought if I could turn pro, it would be worth it. They saw it as a pipe dream. When it became clear that I was headed to the pros, they started paying more attention. I thought finally they loved me. They saw what I had to offer. They came to my games. They cheered." He shook his head. "Then I turned pro, and the money demands, I'm sorry—the money *requests* started. Just a little at first. I gave it to them because they were my parents, and I wanted them to love me. Like a chump."

"You're not a chump for wanting your parents' love. You should expect it."

He shrugged. "It got to the point that all of our conversations centered around money. So-and-so needed money. They wanted to buy a bigger house because surely it's embarrassing for Brady Hudson's parents to live in a 3000-square foot house. Never mind that I'd paid off the mortgage on that 'ridiculously small house.' I did that on my own to say thank you. But it wasn't enough. It was never enough. I finally got the courage to cut them off."

She wrapped her arms around his waist and squeezed. He'd told the story in a matter-of-fact tone with no bitterness, but she knew the situation had killed him. He was still dealing with the scars of their betrayal. "You don't talk to them?"

He shrugged again. "Once every few months. Very stilted conversation. At some point, I get accused of being a bad son for not sending them a blank check, and I hang up the phone."

"But you keep trying."

"Only to a certain extent." A resolute light entered his eyes. "I refuse to let them dictate my actions. I refuse to be used. By anybody." His expression softened, a gentle smile spreading across his normally arrogant face. "That's why I'm lucky to have you. You want me for me with no ulterior motives."

Caitlin pushed her lips upward, hoping he couldn't sense her unrest. She should tell him about Mack. But she couldn't. Not if she wanted him to continue looking at her the way he was. And she did. So much.

Chapter Twelve

"Why the hell am I in Milwaukee?" Brady grumbled the following Wednesday.

"Um, because you have to play the Bucks tomorrow?" Caitlin offered.

He glared at her through the computer screen. "Thanks, smart-ass."

"You're welcome," she said with a grin. "Seriously, though, what's up?"

"I'm bored." He straightened against the bed's headboard, his legs stretched out in front of him, his computer resting on his thighs. His white T-shirt stretched across his chest.

"Why didn't you go out with your teammates?"

"I did. We had dinner, and a few of us came back to watch film. But I kicked them out. Tilly kept talking…chattering. I needed some peace and quiet."

"You're talking to me."

"You're not people. You're Caitlin." He said it like it was obvious. Like she was special and in no way could others compare to her.

Warmth spread through her veins. "What's stopping you from watching more film?"

"Feeling like I know what play the Bucks are going to call before they do. There's only so much film I can watch. I'm just antsy. We haven't played a game in three days, which is weird. I'm ready to go."

She tucked a leg underneath her on her bed. "TV?"

"I thought about watching *The Wire* again, but I've watched the entire series five times. Not in the mood for that tonight. I miss you."

"I miss you, too." And she did. She'd seen him that morning before he left, but that recent visit did nothing to dull the sensation that a part of her was missing. She bit her lip as an idea occurred to her. Could she do it? Did she have the nerve? "I can think of something that won't bore you."

His brows lifted. "What? Got a pirate joke for me?"

"Not tonight."

"Then what?"

She kept her eyes on him as she wiggled.

His eyes widened. "Are you…?"

She held up her shorts. "Yeah, I am."

"Caitlin?" he croaked. The only way to describe the sound that came out of his mouth.

"It's time to stop dreaming, Brady," she said, looking him dead in the eye. He'd joked about this once before, but she hadn't forgotten. She'd do just about anything for him. She set aside her laptop, making sure the webcam faced her. She rose on her knees and whipped her T-shirt over her head, leaving her clad in a matching blue bra and panty set, and nothing else. "What do you want me to do, Brady?"

His gaze swept her figure, missing nothing. She felt the look like a caress. His eyes darkened. "Do you trust me to make you feel good?" His voice had deepened.

"Yes," she said simply. Calmly.

"Take off the bra."

Her eyes trained squarely on his, she reached behind her. A second later, she drew the bra down her arms. "Now what?"

He didn't answer right away. "I love your body." His eyes traced every curve. "Your breasts. Your hips. Your skin. I wish I was there to lick you all over."

A tremor of desire coursed through her at the erotic promise. "Next time."

"Count on it. Your breasts always taste so good. I love when your nipples go hard in my mouth. Touch yourself."

"Where?" She grazed her neck and shoulders with the tips of her fingers. "Here?"

"Lower."

Her fingers slipped to the upper slopes of her breasts. Skimming the skin there. Tracing the outline of the mounds.

"Don't play with me, Caitlin."

Her nipples tightened at the command in his voice.

His tone went amused. "You like that, huh? Looks like a certain part of you doesn't like all your teasing. Touch your nipples, Caitlin. Imagine it's me doing it."

Her eyes fluttered closed, his words washing over her. Like they had a mind of their own, her fingers wandered the few inches south and touched her hard nipples. A shaky moan slipped through her lips at the first contact. A delicious dart of desire lined its way between her legs. Brady loved touching her breasts, playing with them, sucking them. She loved when he did it.

"Just like that, baby," he murmured.

She rolled her right nipple between her index and middle fingers. She pinched her left nipple with her other hand. Ribbons of lust unfurled in her. Her legs pressed together in a doomed attempt to control the arousal rampaging through her system. "Brady."

"Don't close yourself off from me. I want to see everything.

Take off your panties."

She stood on shaky legs only long enough to do as he'd demanded, then lay back on the bed and opened her legs for his view only. She was wet, her inner thighs slippery with want. He could see everything. How wet she was. How close she was. She hid nothing from him. She couldn't even if she wanted to. He saw her. He got her.

His voice, dark and compelling, washed over her. "That's what I want to see. It's time. Touch yourself."

She needed no further direction. Her hand slipped down to the area between her legs. She found her clit, which was begging for mercy, and squeezed. A flood of heat rippled through her. She felt so empty. She needed relief. But only at his direction. Her eyes opened. The fire in his eyes scalded her. She licked her lips, forced them open. "I need you, Brady."

"I know, baby, but you're going to do this by yourself. Go ahead."

Caitlin slipped a finger inside her, her flesh eagerly clamping around the digit. She pumped once, twice, but it wasn't enough, so she added another finger, scraping across her nerve endings. A little better. She settled into an intoxicating rhythm, her bliss just out of reach. Wanting it to be him filling her. She moved her hips in counterpoint to her fingers, wanting to make it good for him. Sending a new wave of pleasure through her system in the process.

A garbled groan had her eyes flying to the computer screen. Brady's chest heaved like he'd just completed five wind sprints in a row, his wild eyes focused on her. She did this to him. She added a third finger, stretching herself. Adding to her pleasure. Yes. That. So good. Too good.

Caitlin gasped. Brady's answering groan let her know her actions were appreciated. Her clit was begging for attention, so she circled it again with her free hand, teasing herself.

Pleasure twisted inside her, tighter and tighter, until she

started to shake with the need to hold it in check. She was so close.

His voice washed over her. "Do you like me watching you pleasure yourself?"

"Yes," she moaned, pressing a finger against her clit.

"Come for me, Caitlin."

She did, the orgasm sweeping through her body, over and over in undulating waves. When the shaking finally stopped, she drew in a breath. "Thank you."

"It was my pleasure, believe me."

Maybe, but he looked tortured, his eyes wild, his mouth drawn tight, his chest still heaving. She drew up, curling her legs behind her. "It's your turn."

His eyes darkened. "What do you want me to do, Caitlin?"

"Do you trust me to make you feel good?"

"Yes," Brady said simply. Calmly.

"Take off your clothes."

He whipped his T-shirt and shorts off.

"Man, I love your body." Her eyes slipped down his frame, boldly leaving no doubt to the truthfulness of her statement. She stopped at his erection and licked her lips. "Especially that part."

His cock jumped like an eager puppy waiting for a treat.

"Did I cause that?" she asked.

"You know you did." He'd nearly gone off like a rocket earlier, but he hadn't wanted anything to distract him from watching Caitlin find her pleasure.

Her lips curled into a magnificent, wicked grin. "Good."

"I can't wait until I see you in person. I'm going to make you pay."

"Promises, promises. Don't you think you should take

care of that first?"

Holding her gaze, he wet his palm with some pre-come seeping out of his dick and then grabbed himself. Taking care of himself was nothing new, but having Caitlin's hot, covetous eyes on him, knowing she could look, but not touch, ramped up the eroticism about ten notches. He pulled hard, the way he liked, the action sending a fresh wave of arousal through him. He gritted his teeth. Tingles crept up his spine, then spread to all corners of his body.

"Keep going," she murmured.

He did. He worked harder. He squeezed. He was rough. He used both hands. His balls drew tight as he reached close to the end. He alternated his strokes, harder, then softer, trying to prolong the ecstasy. The agony.

"I wish it was my hand, my mouth on you. Licking you. Sucking you. Taking you all."

Shit. Was she trying to kill him? Caitlin's mouth was pure magic. Remembering her pleasuring him—how she looked on her knees, how she made him feel when she put her talented lips and tongue to work on him, the sensual look in her eyes— was his undoing. He came with a hoarse grunt, stars exploding behind his eyes.

Sometime later, when he returned to Earth, he immediately sought out his computer screen. Caitlin watched him with a satisfied-with-herself grin on her face. She'd covered that magnificent body of hers with a sheet. Too bad. He'd never get tired of seeing it, worshipping it.

"Hey, stranger," she said. Her eyes slipped down to where he had softened, but was getting harder under her perusal.

"Hold that thought." He gathered the strength to rise from the bed and head for the bathroom.

"Hmm, the back view is almost as nice as the front. Tight, round ass." She let out a wolf whistle.

Brady stopped in his tracks and looked over his shoulder

at the computer. "Are you objectifying me?"

"Yes." She nodded eagerly.

He grinned and continued on his way. He grabbed a towel and cleaned himself up, then returned to the bedroom and drew up his shorts.

"You don't have to do that for my benefit," she said.

"I'm doing it for myself. That was…"

"Incredible?"

"Yeah, for starters. I can honestly say I'm no longer bored."

She laughed, unabashedly. Freely. Like she did everything. Holding nothing back. Her eyes sparkled. Her skin was radiant. She was radiant. So caring. So giving. So Caitlin.

"I love you." The words slipped out before he could stop them. He didn't want to anyway. They were the truth. She made him feel again. Made him realize that he could let people in. He didn't have to hold people responsible for what others had done to him. He was so lucky to have her. The decision to pull over to help her was the best decision of his life.

Her laughter cut off abruptly. Her eyes widened. "What did you say?"

"I said I love you. You're everything I've been looking for and never knew I wanted."

She blinked. "That's, that's—"

"I don't expect you to say it back. At least not yet. But you will."

"I will, will I?"

He'd never been surer of anything in his life. "Yeah. I'm done pretending you don't mean the world to me. Our relationship might have started out as a means to an end, but we've moved so far past that. What we have is the truth."

A smile, stunning, spread across her face like she could no longer contain it. Like she had no desire to do so. She pressed her fingertips to her computer screen like she could actually touch him and trace his features. Her eyes shone with joy. "Why the hell are you in Milwaukee?"

Caitlin moved back and forth in front of her desk. Stupid office. It was way too small for pacing, but it was all she had at the moment, so she'd have to make do. For at least the tenth time, she reached the end of the room and turned and headed for the other side.

"Caitlin?" Noelle asked. "Are you going to tell me what's up? The room isn't that big. I would think the pacing would get old after a while."

She stopped mid-step and faced her best friend. Noelle was perched on the edge of her desk, the concern in her eyes belying her light tone. "Brady said he loves me."

And hearing the words, remembering how he looked when he said it, sent her pacing again.

"Oh." Noelle sounded stunned. "That was fast, but okay. Seems like it was only yesterday that you were telling me y'all had decided to take your relationship from fake to real."

"I know, right? At first, I was shocked, then he said some really sweet things, and I was all 'aww.' Now I'm freaking out."

"I assume by the way you're acting that you don't feel the same way."

She stopped again. "No. Yes. I don't know. He's so not what I thought I wanted except he is. We're so good together, and I care about him. A lot. But to say 'love,' you know that takes a lot for me."

"Is he pressuring you to say you love him?"

"What? No."

"Then what's bothering you? Something obviously is."

Caitlin flopped down in a chair and buried her face in her

hands for a second. "I'm keeping something from him."

Noelle settled in the matching chair. "From me, too, I'm assuming, because I have no idea what you're talking about."

"You're right." She took a deep breath. "I found my father."

Noelle's mouth dropped open. "You did? How?"

"I found a letter he wrote my mom. He's Mack Jameson."

Noelle's eyebrows did their best to leap off her face. "As in the Stampede coach?"

"Yes."

"Wow." Noelle reached for her hand and squeezed. "How are you handling this? Are you okay?"

"Yes, I'm fine. I've had some time to adjust."

Noelle studied her for a second, then nodded. "Okay, but what else aren't you telling me?"

Noelle was her best friend for a reason. She could read her like a book. "I wanted to get close to Mack to get some intel to expose what a fraud he is, which is the real reason I agreed to pretend to date Brady. I planned to write a scathing tell-all column and publish it on Zach Brantley's website."

"Wow. Okay. This is a lot to take in."

"It is, and I know you're going to say that wasn't the healthiest way to handle the situation."

Noelle sighed. "Which is why you didn't tell me."

"Which is why I didn't tell you."

"Is it too optimistic to assume you're having second thoughts?"

"I don't like lying to Brady. I have conflicted feelings about Mack. Brady loves him, and from what I can tell, he's been great for Brady. But I can't forget the hard times growing up. I can't forget how he abandoned my mom without a second thought." She took a deep breath. "But blindsiding him like this doesn't feel right either. I'm finally ready to admit that. The column is finished, but I haven't been able to press send.

I kept telling myself it needed tweaking, but that wasn't it."

"So what are you going to do?"

"The only thing I can do. Confess and hope Brady doesn't hate me." She looked down at her hands for a second. "Do you think he's going to hate me?" Her voice wobbled. "I don't want him to hate me. His last girlfriend used him to get a job and slept with his teammate. I know it wasn't easy for him to trust again after that, and I've been lying to him the whole time."

Noelle drew her into a hug. "Based on what you just said, it couldn't have been easy for him to open up to you. His feelings have to be real. Believe in what he's told and shown you."

Caitlin nodded. "Okay, I'm going to be brave and tell him everything."

But first she had a call to make. After Noelle left, she picked up her phone. "Zach, it's Caitlin Monroe. There's not going to be a story. I changed my mind."

He heaved a sigh. "We didn't sign a contract, so I can't make you change your mind. Whatever it is, it's going to get out if it's as juicy as you claimed. By not publishing the story, you won't be able to control the narrative."

"I'm willing to take that risk. Good-bye." She hung up the phone with no regrets. She was going to handle this her way.

"Hey, Caitlin, where's the recipe for the team cookbook?" Brady asked.

"It's on my desk," she called out from her kitchen.

He looked askance at the desk that was covered with piles of paper and God-only-knew-what-else. That desk? He hefted himself off the sofa and crossed the room. Caitlin claimed she had a system, so he didn't want to mess anything up. He'd been down that road before and rousing the ire of the five-foot-two dynamo wasn't something he wanted to encounter again anytime soon. Though she'd looked cute fussing at him. Sexy.

At least she'd agreed to be a part of the cookbook, which had to mean she saw a future for them. Just because she hadn't told him she loved him didn't mean she didn't or wouldn't. She was skittish. He got that. So patient he would be.

He lifted the stacks gingerly. No recipe. At least not for a German chocolate cake. All manners of articles about people doing weird things, which he could only assume was research for the radio show.

He almost missed it. He'd picked up the pace looking for a single sheet of paper when what he'd seen registered in his brain. He picked up the file folder and opened it. His heart sank. His hopes. His dreams. Everything.

"What the hell is this?"

Brady's seething voice came from behind her. She spun away from the stove where she was carefully frosting the sugar cookies Brady liked so much. She'd been tinkering with the recipe and thought they were her best batch so far. But all those happy thoughts drifted away to nothingness when she registered the look on his face. And the folder in his hand.

"Where did you get that?" she asked. Although she already knew the answer. The place she'd told him to look.

"Why do you have a folder of articles about Mack? Why do you have a background check on him? A very thorough one as far as I can tell. That must have set you back a pretty penny."

"I can explain." She gripped the frosting piping bag in

her hand so hard frosting dripped out onto the counter. She set the bag down carefully to give herself a second to gather her thoughts. She didn't make a move toward Brady. The fire blazing from his eyes let her know it wouldn't be welcome.

"I can't wait to hear it." Sarcasm, so poisoned, so sharp, dripped from his tone.

"Mack is my father."

He shook his head, uncomprehending like she'd started speaking Japanese. "What did you say? What are you talking about?"

"He's my father. He doesn't know," she continued at Brady's mystified look. "I only found out a few weeks ago."

"What were you planning on doing with that info? Don't try to play me for a fool. If you'd planned to have a happy father-daughter reunion, you would have done it already. And that's not even including all the notes in the margin— *Use this. Make sure you tell him that.* Who the hell is he? Because it sure as hell isn't me." He flipped to the front of the folder and pulled out another sheet of paper. "*He's not the man everyone applauds him for being. And that makes him worse. That false facade he shows to the world when the real man is as ugly inside as it gets.* You wrote this drive-by piece." His disgust was real. Palpable.

Even though her heart was threatening to leap out of her chest, she had to remain calm. Make him understand. "I planned to write a column exposing him for the liar he is. He got my mom pregnant, wrote her a check for five thousand dollars, and told her he never wanted to see her again."

"You never planned to talk to him about it, I guess. It's not like you didn't have the opportunity to talk to him. Instead you planned to sell your story to the highest bidder."

She swallowed. "That was the plan, yes."

"Let me guess. Mommy Dearest put you up to this."

Her chin lifted. "No, my mother knows nothing about it."

"Aww, I see. You thought you'd get in her good graces with your act of bravery." He sniffed, shook his head. "Where do I fit in all of this?"

She went to him then. "I care about you. You know that."

He wrenched his arm away. "I don't know anything. Was this all a set-up?"

"No."

"No, but when you saw a golden opportunity, you ran with it, right? Tell me I'm lying, Caitlin. Tell me that you didn't use me to get closer to your father. Tell me."

Tears gathered in her eyes. "I can't, but let me explain."

"I don't want to hear it. What a damn fool I was. 'Reel him in even more,' I'm sure you said. You must have been crowing when I told you I loved you. I'm sure you told yourself 'Now he won't be able to let me go and I can get closer to Mack.'" He backed away, his eyes widening. "Is that why you were so eager to accept that invitation to his house? So eager to cook with him?"

She didn't say anything. What was there to say?

He continued moving away. "You're just like all the others. I should have known it was too good to be true. I should have known you were too good to be true. Everyone always is. I thought I had to give you time. But that wasn't it at all. You didn't give a damn at all. It was all a game to you."

"Brady, please listen to me. What I feel for you is real. What we have is the truth. You told me that."

"How the hell am I supposed to believe that when you've been lying to me the whole time? Using me?"

She went to him. Flinched when he again rejected her touch. "Listen to me. I changed my mind. I'm not publishing the column."

"Mighty convenient now that I found out, especially when I have the proof in my hands. You liked writing this. I can tell by the tone of the piece."

His disgust was too much for her to take. Her frustration boiled over. "Yes, I did! Everyone thinks he's perfect when he's anything but."

"Listen to yourself. You're so poisoned you don't care who you hurt in your thirst for revenge and need to make Mommy love you. Grow the fuck up, Caitlin. You're an adult and control what you do."

His words, his tone, stunned her. Blasted her. She retreated. He didn't know the heartache, the confusion, the cold nights wondering if they'd find enough money for food, let alone to pay the rent. "If you can't see why this was important to me, then we don't have anything else to say to each other."

His cold eyes bit into her. "We don't."

He turned on his heel. A few seconds later, the front door slammed. The sudden silence nearly suffocated her.

Chapter Thirteen

"Caitlin, honey, what's wrong?" her mom asked.

Rocking side to side, Caitlin pushed a hand through her hair. "I need to talk to you. I have two things to say."

"Okay. Come in." Her mom guided her inside with a hand at her elbow.

They settled on the sofa in the living room. Good. Caitlin didn't think her weight could support her any longer.

"What's this about?"

"I know." The words burst from her with the speed of a torpedo. She'd been holding them back for so long.

Her mom frowned. "Know what?"

"Who my father is."

"Wh-what are you talking about?" Her mother spoke slowly, haltingly, like she was struggling to remember how to form words.

"I know that Mack Jameson is my father."

Her mom fell back against the sofa cushion. "What? How?"

"When I was cleaning out your closet to get the clothes to donate a few weeks ago, I found the letter he wrote you."

"Oh." Her mother, always so self-assured, always such a steady presence, looked shell-shocked. Her hands shook in her lap until she noticed Caitlin watching, then she balled them into fists. "Why didn't you say anything?"

"The letter made me so mad. I planned to confront and humiliate him in front of all his colleagues the night I met Brady. But I couldn't go through with it, and I was embarrassed by my cowardice. All I wanted to do was make you proud of me, and I couldn't go through with it. What kind of daughter was I if I couldn't confront the jerk who would've preferred that I'd never been born?"

"Oh, honey, you would have been who you've always been—the kindhearted daughter who never likes to cause anyone distress and who always tries to boost others' spirits. The one who cracks jokes to keep everyone laughing."

Caitlin rejected the kind words with a shake of her head. "But what he did to you—"

"Was horrible, but I have the two best kids a mother could ever hope to have."

"I've never lived up to your expectations."

Her mother wrapped an arm around Caitlin, who snuggled into the embrace, the familiar scent of her mom's favorite perfume comforting her. "What are you talking about? I've always been proud of you. Yes, I push you, but only because I never want you to settle. There's greatness inside of you, and sometimes I feel like *you* don't see it. You're so busy trying to please others that you don't concentrate on what you want and everything you've accomplished."

"You gave me and Chris such a great life. I wanted to repay you. I didn't want to be a disappointment."

"Oh, honey. I've never expected you to be perfect. How can I when I'm far from it?"

Caitlin gaped at her mother. "What are you talking about? You raised us on your own. Kept food on the table all by yourself. Made sure we stayed on the straight and narrow. Went to law school."

"I did, and it wasn't easy. It would've been easier if I hadn't let my pride get in the way and taken your father to court. Yes, he wrote that letter and check, but there was no reason that had to be the end of it. I had the law on my side. Pride and embarrassment kept me from going after him, which wasn't fair to you and your brother, but it's proof that I'm not perfect. I don't expect you to be perfect either. I just want you to fight for what you want. Will you make mistakes? Of course. We all do. But I will *always* be proud of you."

Caitlin nodded, hearing the truth in the words. Accepting them for the first time in her life. "Since we're on the subject, you should know that I'm happy being a radio producer. It's challenging work, and I can't imagine doing anything else, including being the host of the show."

Miranda chuckled. "That's my daughter I know and love." Her smile slipped away. "Does Christian know?"

"Yes," Caitlin admitted.

She threw her hands up in the air. "Lord, you two, always keeping secrets and using twin-speak to communicate. Always did right from the start. I've never been happier or more scared the day y'all were born. I guess this explains why I haven't heard much from him lately."

Caitlin exchanged a look with her mother. He always needed time to process upsetting news on his own. It was frustrating, but something they'd both come to accept over the years.

She asked a question that had been weighing on her mind. "Are you still in love with Mack?"

"Mack is a footnote in my life, nothing more. Any love I felt for him died a quick death when I read that letter." Her mom squeezed her hand. "Speaking of the men in our lives, how does Brady come into this?"

Caitlin drew back her shoulders. "That's the other thing I came to say. I'm not giving him up. He and I are a package deal, so you're going to have to accept him." The tears she'd been so determined not to shed welled up. "Oh, Mama. I screwed up. I hurt him, and he'll never be able to forgive me."

"I'm sure that's not true."

"It is. I told him I'd pretend to date him knowing I planned to use our time together to gather dirt on Mack. And he found out." A loud sob escaped.

Her mother gathered her in her arms again. "Shh. Honey, it will be okay. Usually, things aren't as bad as they seem."

Caitlin wiped her eyes. "I love him so much."

"I know."

The calm assertion stunned her. "How? I just realized it myself."

"I knew when I saw the way you looked at him the day you bought your car. I knew he couldn't be all bad if he could convince you to get rid of that rattletrap, something no one else was able to do. I knew he was in love with you when he politely, but very clearly, put me in my place at dinner."

Caitlin chuckled through her tears. "So you're not going to tell me I'm making a mistake?"

"Will you listen if I do?"

"No."

Her mom laughed. "That's my girl. I'm never going to stop worrying about you. That's a mother's job. But it's clear to me now that you're an adult and know your own heart and mind."

"But what if I can't get him to change his mind?"

Her mom scoffed. "You're Caitlin Monroe. He doesn't stand a chance of resisting you."

"I love you, Mama."

"Love you too, honey."

Caitlin stared at the door like a pit of vipers waited on the other side.

"You can go on in. He's expecting you," the admin assistant said.

Caitlin sent a small smile over her shoulder, knocked, and opened the door with a shaky hand. She was here because of Brady. While she'd been urging him to change, it was really her who needed to change. To learn how to forgive.

"Caitlin, nice to see you again," Mack said, looking up from the clipboard in his hand. He stood. "What brings you by?"

"I need to talk to you."

He held out a hand, inviting her to sit. "About Brady? Is everything okay?"

"I'd prefer to stand, and yes, Brady's fine." She assumed. She hoped. She hadn't seen or heard from him other than the glimpses she got on TV in two days. "I'm not here because of him."

"Then what can I do for you?"

She'd rehearsed her speech a million times. "About thirty years ago, you wrote a letter to a woman pregnant with your child and essentially told her to get lost. I'm that child. One of them at least."

The clipboard fell out of his hand, clattering on his desk. "Wh-what are you talking about?"

She looked him dead in the eye. "You know very well what I'm talking about. My mother is Miranda Monroe."

The recognition of the name dawned on his face. "I...I don't know what to say."

Caitlin wanted to say something sarcastic, but the pure

shock on his face stopped her. Instead, she dropped into the chair in front of his desk with a sigh. "Why don't you start at the beginning? Why did you lead my mom on only to leave her in the dust?"

He studied her. She met his gaze unflinchingly. After a few seconds, he nodded and sat. "I won't sugarcoat the facts. I was young. And foolish. And selfish. I had the whole world at my feet. The money, the fame was coming at me in a rush, and I loved it. I didn't want anything slowing me down."

"You mean someone, not anything."

He acknowledged her correction with a small nod. "I told myself that she was trying to trap me, and I wasn't going to let that happen." He shook his head. "I was twenty years old. I thought something better was around the corner. I tried my best to not think about your mom and what decision she chose to make. I assumed she had an abortion. That was easier than thinking I had a child out there. I never thought about it. I refused to."

"Two children. Don't forget I have a twin brother."

He winced. A combination of regret and pain settled on his face. "Oh my God. I'm so sorry. How long have you known?"

"A few weeks. The plan was to expose you in a tell-all column on a gossip site."

He didn't look shocked or angry. "I would have deserved it. You said that *was* the plan. And now?"

Caitlin lifted her chin. "I can't do it. I'm not as bloodthirsty as I thought I was. Exposing you like that to the world is distasteful to me. That's not who I am or what I want to be known for. What would it accomplish?"

"Thank you," he said simply.

Her voice hardened. "I want you to know that I don't regret writing it. I needed to get it all out. But ultimately it was for my eyes only. To help me reconcile my jumbled up emotions."

He nodded.

"I also want you to know I had the best mom ever who did whatever she needed to do to provide for her kids and make sure we had a happy home."

His lips lifted in a small smile. "In the little time I've spent with you, I can tell she did a great job. This probably won't mean much to you, but when I got married, I did so with the promise to be a better man. I couldn't rewrite history, but I could do my best going forward." He hesitated. "It's presumptuous of me to ask, but I'd like to get to know you and your brother. I can't change what I did, but we can always steer our future."

It was her turn to study him. "I wanted to hate you. I was convinced the nice-guy persona was an act. But it isn't."

He clasped his hands together. "I've grown up a lot over the past thirty years. I'd like the chance to prove it to you."

Caitlin took a deep breath. "I've had to do some growing up lately, but I'm starting to get there. We can try."

"Please. I would like that."

"It won't be easy."

"I won't give up, and neither will you. You have the Jameson genes in you. Giving up isn't in your DNA."

She offered up a small smile.

Mack rose and walked around the desk to sit next to her. "At some point in time, after we've gotten to know each other and only if you're comfortable doing so, how would you feel about issuing a joint statement about our relationship? I would like to acknowledge you and your brother publicly. I don't want it to be a dirty secret people whisper about in corners."

She nodded. "Because it will come to light at some point. Although I'm not publishing the story, I'm sure the owner of the site will dig trying to figure it out. My brother and I aren't a dirty little secret. You're right. We want to control the story. Maybe you can come on the radio show. Noelle, the host, is my best friend."

Mack patted her hand. "Good idea. We'll do it when and if the timing is right."

She stared at the connection, tentative, but real. "Sounds like a plan."

"Speaking of people finding out, does Brady know?" Mack asked.

Her lips downturned. "He just found out, and he's not speaking to me. He thinks I was using him to get to you and that my feelings for him aren't genuine."

"But they are."

"Yes, they are." She straightened in the chair. "Like you said, I have the Jameson genes in me, but I was molded by Miranda Monroe, so I'm going to be bold and ask for a favor."

"Anything you want."

Eight seconds left on the game clock. The Stampede were down one, but they had the ball. Time to make something happen. Time to make the home crowd go wild. Time to make their long-time rivals, the Spurs, head back to San Antonio on an unhappy flight.

A situation Brady always thrived on. Always. This is why he played the game. He wasn't proud or happy to admit that his attention this game had sucked. The court was always his sanctuary. No matter what craziness was going on in his personal life, he could always count on going onto the court and forgetting it all for a couple of hours.

But today had been different. He'd missed some easy shots, some easy passes. His miscues hadn't cost them the game. Not yet anyway. So he needed to concentrate like he hadn't the entire game.

He looked to his coach for last-second instructions. Caitlin's father. He wanted to believe she'd lied to him about her connection to Mack, but now that he knew, it was easy to see. They had the same eyes. How was he supposed to concentrate with that kind of knowledge dangling over his head? Should he tell Mack so he wasn't ambushed by her story or stay the hell out of it? Did Mack deserve to be told if what Caitlin said was the truth?

He'd managed to resist looking into the stands the entire game. He'd become much too comfortable looking up for the support Caitlin always lent him. She wouldn't be there anyway. He wouldn't want her to be. She'd lied to him. Betrayed him. Used him.

But his eyes, independent of his brain, looked into the crowd. And there she was looking as beautiful as ever, sitting on the edge of her seat, like she couldn't wait for the game to resume, hoping the Stampede would pull out a victory.

Excitement zoomed through him. No. What the hell was she doing here? Who'd given her a ticket to sit in the family section? Did she think he would forgive and forget with a snap of his fingers?

"All right," Mack said, interrupting his thoughts. "This is what we're going to do." The coach drew up the play on his whiteboard. Brady barely needed to look at the drawing. It was their bread-and-butter play, the one they worked on in practice constantly, although Mack didn't call it often in games. He didn't want teams sitting on it, but this was a special occasion. Division rival with first place on the line.

Tilly would throw the ball in to Brady, and he and Maguire would work the pick and roll to get Maguire an open shot.

The whistle blew. Execution time. No more time to think about Caitlin and why she was here. Brady and his teammates took their spots on the court. Tilly threw the ball in. Brady dribbled and surveyed the court while a shot clock played in his head. Maguire worked the pick and roll like he was supposed to. The Spurs weren't making it easy, bodying up on Maguire, but Brady was still able to get him the ball.

Three seconds.

No one was more surprised than he was when the ball came winging back to him. His instincts took over. He squared up and took the shot. The ball swished through the net as the buzzer went off.

Game over.

The Stampede had won. Purple and white streamers poured down from the ceiling. The crowd roared. Brady turned in a circle to take it all in. This is why he played. This is what he loved. Basketball, as challenging as it could be, never let him down. Not like people. The game was always the same. It was always there for him.

And then he couldn't see anything at all because his teammates mobbed him. Someone jumped on his back. Someone else slapped him on the head. Laughing, he braced himself as best as he could against the onslaught.

A few seconds later, the pile broke up, and he exchanged a high-five with Tilly. The team's public relations director handed him a pair of headphones and pointed him to the scorer's table for the postgame interview with the local TV crew.

"Brady, you had a tough game until the last shot," the play-by-play announcer said.

He nodded. "Yeah, that happens sometimes. You have to keep fighting until the last second."

"It didn't look like that last play was designed to go to you."

"No, it wasn't, but the Spurs had it covered well. Luckily, Maguire saw that I was open and passed the ball to me. I'm just glad it went in."

"Your teammates mobbed you afterward. That must have felt good. You really seem to be settling in with the team after some bumpiness in the early going."

"I am. I won't lie. Coming here was an adjustment after being in New York for so long, but the team is really coming together. I can't wait to see where we end up. The future is bright."

After the interviewer thanked him for joining the postgame show, Brady took off the headphones and ran off the court, high-fiving fans.

When he jogged into the locker room, he froze. Why wasn't there any music playing? Why wasn't anyone celebrating the fact that they'd just won the biggest game of the year?

"Hello," he called out. "Was I the only one out there?"

His teammates turned to him one by one. Then they all bum-rushed him. The music started blaring. The celebration was on.

"Gentlemen, how are we going to celebrate tonight's epic victory?" Tilly asked after the reporters had cleared out.

"I'm in the mood to watch the game-winning play and the look on the Spurs' faces over and over again," Whitmore said.

"We can do that at my place," Brady heard himself say. "I live across the street, so it'll only take a minute to get there."

"Sounds like a plan, especially if you have a refrigerator full of beer," Tilly said.

"That can be arranged."

Ten minutes later, Brady exited the locker room with his teammates.

"Dude, you live across the street from the arena," Tilly said when they arrived at Brady's condo. "This should have been the designated spot to chill the day you were traded here." The players liked to find places where they could unwind without having to worry about being on for fans.

"Well, we're here now, so let's do this," Victor said. "Is that a pool table I see?" He and Tilly walked over to the table with a few players in tow.

A few others wandered over to his bookshelf to check out his Blu-Ray collection.

Brady headed to the kitchen. His teammates were having a good time, so he should be happy. They'd won an important game. So why was he staring into his refrigerator like it held the secrets of the universe inside? Because he felt like a part of him was missing.

"Yo, dude, you gonna bring out any beers or what?" Whitmore said from behind him.

"Yeah, yeah, I got it," Brady said, grabbing two cans. He passed one to his teammate and popped the top on the other one.

"Thanks." Whitmore turned on his heel and exited the kitchen.

Maguire joined him in the kitchen. "You got any food?"

"The fridge is yours."

"Thanks." Maguire studied the contents of the refrigerator for a few seconds before closing the door. "Hey, man, I didn't say anything earlier, but thanks for taking the blame for what happened in New York. My fiancée would have killed me."

Brady grunted. "The league looked into it and determined I wasn't at fault, so it turned out all right."

"I know, but it was still a stand-up thing to do. The media were all over you, and you never cracked. I appreciate it."

"Is that why you passed the ball to me tonight?"

"Yeah, and also because you were open." Maguire looked away for a second. "Look, I've been acting like an ass because my best friend got traded away, and I wanted to say I'm sorry."

The apology stunned him. Then it warmed his heart.

"Apology accepted." Brady slapped him on the chest and headed back to the game room. His teammates were gathered around the TV watching the highlights on SportsCenter for the umpteenth time.

"Hey, where's your lady?" Tilly asked. "I'd think you'd want to be celebrating with her instead of us. I mean I would if she was my girl."

"Watch it," Brady said. "We're done."

"What? I heard y'all on the radio. I've never felt the need to throw up as much as when I was listening to you moon over each other."

Brady's jaw clenched. "She lied to me, okay?"

"And?"

"What do you mean 'and'? Isn't that enough?"

Tilly shrugged. "It can be, but not always. What did she lie about?"

"Something pretty damned important." Brady downed his beer, the words tasting more bitter than the alcohol.

"So that's it?"

"What do you mean 'so that's it'? She kept something from me."

Tilly looked at him like he'd lost his mind. "So you've told her your every dirty secret, huh?"

"No, but what she did—"

"Listen to me, man," Victor interrupted. "I've been married a long time and have learned a few things. People aren't perfect, but that doesn't mean they're not worth keeping in your life. Sometimes you have to trust in that. Nobody is perfect and expecting them to be will lead nowhere fast."

"I'm done talking about this. We can play pool or you can all get the hell out." Brady stalked away.

His teammates dropped the subject, but the mood in the condo was altered, and the party broke up less than an hour later.

"I don't know what's going on between you and Caitlin, but I do know you became less of an ass when she showed up." Tilly offered those parting words on his way out.

It hit him as he locked the door and confronted the silence now permeating his condo. His teammates gave a shit about him and what was going on in his life outside the basketball court. And he cared about them. A month ago, he never would have confided in them, and they sure as hell wouldn't have asked what was bothering him. They'd bonded. None of that would've happened without Caitlin.

He was a better person for having her in his life. Could he take their advice? Put aside his own feelings of betrayal and go after the woman who'd come to mean so much to him in such a short period of time? Could he trust that what they had was indeed the truth? Did he really want to spend the rest of his life without the woman he loved because of his pride?

Chapter Fourteen

Caitlin took a deep breath and knocked. When the door opened, she ignored her racing heart and pasted on a smile. "Hi, Brady," she said cheerfully. "Sorry to stop by so late, but great game tonight." She pushed the plastic-wrapped plate into his chest until he was forced to take it and used the distraction to slip by him into his condo.

Okay, good. She'd made it inside. She'd failed miserably earlier in the night at the game, unable to force herself to go to the locker room. He'd looked so happy after making the winning shot, she hadn't wanted to bring his mood down. But she'd regrouped. Had given herself a pep talk. She was made of stern stuff. She hoped.

He hadn't slammed the door in her face. That didn't mean he couldn't literally pick her up and throw her out if he wanted to. She moved deeper into the condo. No need to make it easy for him.

He shut the door and faced her. "What are you doing here?" His voice, his body language, betrayed nothing.

"I made you some sugar cookies. Your favorite."

He stared at the plate like he'd forgotten he was holding it. "I see."

"But that's not the main reason I'm here. We need to talk. Actually, no, I need to talk." His expression didn't change. Okay, so he wasn't happy to see her. Not unexpected, but she could do this. She had to. The panic threatening to close her air passageway would not win. Not today.

A torrent of words came pouring out of her. "I was going to wait until tomorrow, but I couldn't. I have something to say and you're going to listen to me." She paced, lost in all she'd planned to say. She had to get it all out before he threw her out. She had to get through to him. "I'm so sorry for what I did."

"I know."

"It was stupid and not well thought out, but it in no way impacted how I feel about you and us."

"I know."

She reached the window that offered a view of downtown Dallas and turned back toward him. "Please forgive me. No, I'm not asking. You *have* to forgive me."

"I know."

"Because I love you, and I know you don't believe me, but I do. I'm not giving you up. I won't let you give up on me, on us."

"I know."

"What we have is too rare to give up on."

"Caitlin!"

She jumped about three feet in the air. "Huh? What?"

"I know!"

She stopped pacing, his words, his voice finally penetrating her single-minded focus. "You know?"

A heart-melting smile spread across the face of the man who meant the world to her. "I know."

"Which part?"

"All of it."

"You…do?" she whispered, afraid to believe it.

He nodded solemnly and crossed the room, his gaze focused squarely on her. "I don't let people in easily."

"I know."

"Not the extent of it. My parents, yeah, they were a problem, but they weren't the only ones. Things started to change when it became obvious I was going pro."

"In college?"

"In high school. People use you. It comes with the territory. I play a team sport, but after a while you realize that people who say they care about you only care about what you can do for them. It got to the point that I pushed everyone away, including my teammates. I thought I was going to marry my last girlfriend. She knew I didn't trust easily, and she used that knowledge to reel me in, always doing just enough to make me trust a little more. I didn't realize what was going on until it was too late. I now realize it was all a game to her. Not real. I got traded right after all that happened. I wasn't in a good place. Then I met you, and you challenged everything I knew. Everything I thought I knew about people. I started to trust again."

She looked down. "But then I let you down."

He lifted her chin. "I put too much pressure on you to be perfect. You were my shining beacon and that wasn't fair to you."

"What I did wasn't nice."

"And you feel bad about it."

"I do."

"That's why I love you."

She squinted. "You love me because I feel bad about myself?"

That heart-stopping grin spread across his face again. "I love you, but not because you feel bad about yourself."

"Then why?"

"Because you have such a capacity for compassion. You're always looking out for other people that I couldn't believe you would do something so underhanded."

"Me either. That's why I couldn't go through with it. The thought that I could cause someone else pain in some crazy attempt to make myself feel better never sat well with me."

"What happened? I'm ready to listen this time, instead of accusing you of horrible things and yelling at you."

"At the beginning, I was so sure I was justified. I was hurt and angry when I found out who my father was and what he did. I saw an opportunity and jumped at it. I never expected you. I thought I had it all figured out. I wasn't going to fall for an athlete. Not after what happened in college and finding out about Mack. I wasn't going to let anyone distract me from my goal." Her lips tugged upward. "But you did. You were kind and considerate and funny and sincere and everything I didn't think I needed. You're the man I fell in love with. I'm so sorry I hurt you."

"I'm sorry I freaked out on you and walked out."

She placed a hand over his chest. His steady heartbeat centered her. Gave her the strength to continue. "I want you to know that I was telling the truth when I said I'd already told the guy who runs the gossip site I couldn't do it when you found that file. Because you taught me that I have to do what is best for me. Not what I think is right for someone else. Not even for my mom. I was telling you to let go of the past when I was the one who needed to follow my own advice. I'm ready to finally put the past behind me and stop trying to make up for my mistakes. I told her she had to be nice to you because I wasn't giving you up."

His smile melted her heart. "I'm glad. I knew you had it in you. You're too tough not to speak your mind eventually."

"My mom wasn't the only one who got a piece of my

mind. I talked to Mack."

"And?"

"He admitted he was an ass back then and he's been trying in his own way to make up for it."

Brady nodded. "I'm not surprised."

"We're going to try to build a relationship."

"You both mean a lot to me, so I'm glad."

"Me, too." Caitlin's nose twitched. "What's that?"

"Wait."

But she was already headed toward the kitchen. Inside the entrance, she halted. On the counter was the homeliest red velvet cake she'd ever seen. Or at least that's what she assumed it was. It really was homely. And lopsided.

Brady wrapped his arms around her waist. She leaned into his embrace and stared at the most beautiful dessert she'd ever seen. "You baked me a cake."

"Yeah, I was putting on the finishing touches when you showed up. I planned to take it to you tonight."

She turned within the circle of his arms. "But I showed up ruining your plans. That's why you weren't jumping for joy when I showed up."

"I was surprised."

"God, what did I do to deserve you?" Tears pricked at her eyes again.

"Hey, hey, none of that. It's not about what you did to deserve me. It's the other way around. You make me a better man, and the past few days have been hell without you. I was so closed off to everyone and thought that was the best way to get through life. And then you came along and refused to let me continue to live that way. You showed me the joy in life."

"I love you."

"I know."

She tapped him on the chest. "Stop saying that."

"Okay, how about this? I love you, Caitlin Monroe, with

all my heart and have no plans to give you up. Ever."

"All right, that's better."

"Oh, man. You know what this means?"

"What?"

"I'm dating someone associated with the team after all."

"It was your destiny."

"No, you were my destiny. Everything I've been through led me straight to you, and I couldn't be happier about it. I can't wait for the next radio show, so I can let everyone know."

Caitlin met him halfway for a kiss. She melted into him, pouring all her love into the embrace. He reciprocated, making her feel more loved and desired than she'd ever felt in her entire life. But it wasn't enough. It never was. The kiss quickly turned incendiary, heat spreading through her flesh. She slipped her hands under his shirt, the need to touch him overwhelming her.

He picked her up and deposited her on the counter. She pressed a string of kisses to the strong line of his throat. "Are we about to deflower another kitchen?"

He made quick work of her shirt and dropped a kiss over her heart. "If I have anything to say about it, then yes."

She grinned. "I suggest you get to it then."

"With pleasure, Ms. Caitlin."

Epilogue

Brady and Caitlin stepped out of the elevator and headed to his front door.

She stopped in front of him, practically bouncing in excitement. "Hey, Brady, guess what?"

He grinned. "What?"

"You're an NBA champion."

"I am, aren't I?" He hadn't stopped smiling since the last seconds ticked away in Game 6 against the Chicago Bulls, and the reality had sunk in. For the first time ever, he could call himself a champion. And it felt about a million times better than he'd ever imagined. The only thing—person—to ever make him feel better stood in front of him.

Adrenaline still coursed through his veins. He felt like he could go play another three games in a row and never run out of energy. It was two a.m., and he didn't give a damn. After the trophy presentation, the team had convened at a club not far from the arena and partied with fans. The best night of his life.

"You sure you didn't want to stay at the club?" she asked, concern filling her eyes.

His teammates were still there and would be until the sun came up. He regretted nothing. "Positive. I couldn't wait to be alone with you. Come here, baby."

She surprised him by jumping into his arms. He caught her with a small *oomph* and a louder laugh. She pressed that tight, curvy body into him, her breasts pushing against his chest. The smell of peaches intoxicated him, as always. She pressed kisses all over his face. "I'm so, so happy for you. No one deserves it more. I love you, Brady."

"I love you, too, but I'd love you more if you did one thing for me."

She leaned back. "What?"

"Kiss my mouth, not my nose and cheeks."

She pretended to ponder his request for a second. "Okay, I guess I can do that."

Her kiss always took him out of his mind, punched him in the gut. This time was no different. He groaned when she ended the kiss.

"Hey, I just had a thought," she said. "Can I get a ring, too? Championship rings are so gaudy and completely ridiculous. I must have one. As a long-suffering fan and an unofficial assistant coach, I think I deserve one."

He set her on her feet. "You do, do you?"

She nodded, her excitement and desire and love for him shining brightly in the brown eyes he'd never get tired of staring into. "I do. So can I have one?"

He unlocked the door. "I'm sure that can be arranged, but…"

"But what?"

He gestured for her to precede him into the condo. Caitlin stepped inside and gasped. Red rose petals covered the floor of his condo. Several candles were lit around the room, casting the room with an aromatic, romantic glow.

"Brady, what's going on?" A tremor had entered her voice.

"I can get you a championship ring, but I'm hoping you'll want to wear another ring instead." He dropped to his knee and pulled out the box he'd been carrying with him all day from his jacket pocket. He flipped it open to reveal a sparkling diamond ring. "I knew when I woke up this morning that I would be a champion by the end of the night and that I'd be asking the most beautiful, most caring woman I've ever known to spend the rest of her life with me." He'd never been surer of anything in his life. "Caitlin Monroe, I love you. Will you do me the honor of becoming my wife and making me the luckiest man on earth?"

She gasped and covered her face with shaking hands. "Thank God you didn't propose to me at the arena."

He laughed. He'd thought about declaring his love in front of nineteen thousand of their closest friends, but he'd known she'd hate it. "No, this was too special a moment, only meant for both of us."

"You know me so well."

He quirked an eyebrow. "I do, which is why I know you're torturing me by not answering my question."

She tapped her chin. "You might be on to something. And also because you already know the answer. Yes, yes, of course I'll marry you!"

His hands shaking, Brady slipped the ring on her finger and rose. He entwined their fingers and drew her to him. "Thank you for making me believe in what I was so sure didn't exist. I'm going to spend the rest of my life proving you right for taking a chance on me."

She pressed a gentle kiss to his mouth that warmed every spot in his body. "This is just the beginning. I can't wait to see what the future holds."

"Pirate jokes and sugar cookies, I hope."

She hugged him tight. "You can count on it."

Acknowledgments

Thank you to every reader who gave a brand-new author a chance. It gives me a thrill every time one of you reaches out to tell me you enjoyed my book. I love writing and sharing my stories with the world. I couldn't do it without you.

I didn't tell most people that I wrote until my first book was published because, to me, there was nothing to tell. To all my family and friends, I love y'all! Thank you so much for all the support after I outed myself. LOL. And please don't take it personally that I didn't tell you.

Thank you Gwen Hayes, my first editor. I love this book, and it wouldn't have happened without you pushing me to come up with the best book I could.

Thank you to my current editor, Tracy Montoya. You took me on sight unread, and it's been a fabulous partnership so far. Your thoughtful edits made this book so much better. Thank you for your patience. Here's to many more books together!

To my writing friends Roni Loren, Dawn Alexander, Genny Wilson, Piper Huguley, Tracey Livesay, the Firebirds, and so many more, thank you, thank you! You keep me entertained. You give me someone to whine to. You understand.

About the Author

Jamie Wesley has been reading romance novels since she was about 12, when her mother left a romance novel, which a friend had given her, on the nightstand. Jamie read it instead, and the rest is history.

She started her first manuscript, a contemporary romance, after she graduated from Northwestern University in 2002 and couldn't find a job. Life got in the way as it often does, i.e. she found a job, and she didn't finish the story. However, she never forgot about it and finally got serious about completing it in 2009. And then she finished a few more stories. In 2012, her manuscript, TELL ME SOMETHING GOOD, was named a finalist in RWA's Golden Heart competition and was published by Entangled Publishing in 2014.

Jamie holds a master's degree in sport management (yes, that's a real thing :-)) from the University of Texas at Austin, so it probably comes as no surprise that she loves sports and spends an inordinate amount of time rooting for her hometown Dallas's pro sports teams and her alma maters.

If you'd like to find out about new releases and get

exclusive excerpts, sign up for Jamie's mailing list here. Jamie can also be found at www.jamiewesley.com.

Twitter: @Jamie_Wesley

Facebook: www.facebook.com/authorjamiewesley

51734314R00133

Made in the USA
Charleston, SC
30 January 2016